Malkın

StarMaker Books by Sophie Masson,
published by Saint Mary's Press:

The First Day
Serafin
Malkin

Other StarMaker Books:

Neighbors and Traitors, by Carole Duncan Buckman

Malkin

Sophie Masson

ST★R Maker **BOOKS**

Saint Mary's Press
Christian Brothers Publications
Winona, Minnesota

Genuine recycled paper with 10% post-consumer waste.
Printed with soy-based ink.

The publishing team included Stephan Nagel, series editor; Laurie A. Berg,
copy editor; Alan S. Hanson, production editor and typesetter; Cären Yang,
cover designer; Cindi Ramm, art director; produced by the graphics divi-
sion of Saint Mary's Press.

Cover images: Stone, Pal Hermansen, background; PhotoDisc, Inc., back-
gound faces; Zefa, Germany, Index Stock, bottom

Copyright © 2000 by Saint Mary's Press, 702 Terrace Heights, Winona, MN
55987-1320. All rights reserved. No part of this book may be reproduced
by any means without the written permission of the publisher.

Printed in the United States of America

Printing: 9 8 7 6 5 4 3 2 1

Year: 2008 07 06 05 04 03 02 01 00

ISBN 0-88489-669-2

Library of Congress Cataloging-in-Publication Data
Masson, Sophie, 1959–
    Malkin / by Sophie Masson.
        p. cm.
"StarMaker Books."
Summary: Based on the traditional English tale, *Tattercoats,* this novel fol-
lows the plight of the beautiful, neglected granddaughter of the Baron of
Fisher Forest and her special friend, Malkin.
    ISBN 0-88489-669-2 (pbk.)
    [1. Fairy tales.] I. Title.
    PZ8.M44845 Mal 2000
    Fic—dc21
                                                        00-008079

Previously published in Australia and New Zealand in 1998 by Hodder
Headline Australia Pty Limited.
Press Pty Ltd, Adelaide

To Amy, Nimneh, and Isatu, with love.
And also for Ray.

Be as thou wast wont to be:
See as thou wast wont to see.

William Shakespeare, *A Midsummer Night's Dream*

Contents

Part One

Field and Forest

» One «

Thud, thud! Malkin put her hands over her ears and hurried down the corridor. She hurried because if anyone saw her, she'd be in trouble. *Bang, crash!* But there was no escaping the sounds. The old Baron of Fisher Forest had brought in builders again, and the castle would be immersed in dust and smoke until they left, like all the other times. Every few weeks for the past three years, the builders would come and change something else about the castle, so that you might go down a corridor you'd always known and find yourself in some place you'd never clapped eyes on before. That was because the latest in a long line of seers, alchemists, and magicians had told the Baron that if he changed everything around, his daughter would return. *Crash, thump!* Oh, that sounded uncommonly like a heavy body crashing to the ground. It was followed by the sound of loud swearing. Malkin grinned to herself. Mafioso, the latest magician, must have had more than a finger in the building trade, she thought, because his divining had certainly brought much work for all the builders both near and far. And it must be admitted that in some respects it had improved the castle, from the vast, draughty, old-fashioned place it had been to almost the latest in fashionable design. But Mafioso's reign was nearing its end; such things always did. Before Mafioso there had been Serena, who had told the Baron that his daughter would be tempted to return only if there were the finest cloths to receive her, the most beautiful tapestries. Weavers and spinners and dyers of all shapes and sizes and descriptions had turned up at the castle, some honest but most rogues of the most blatant kind. They had finally been sent packing by the furious, grief-stricken Baron, leaving yards and yards of coarse and fine cloth behind them, cloth the Baron had not even wanted to look at before he retired once again to his tower room, there to weep and consult his magic dictionaries and almanacs and grow more of the beard that yearly crept down his massive but wasted frame.

Before Serena there had been the alchemist Truefew, who had vowed that the Baron's daughter would only be restored if the Baron were able to find the Worldstone, which cured all ills and brought the dead back to life. To find this stone, you had to use much gold—much, much gold—melted down and refined, its essence captured so as to hold the elusive Worldstone. Alas! Much gold had indeed gone, vaporized into essence, but the Worldstone had remained elusive. Truefew had not waited to be sent packing, he had mysteriously vaporized himself one morning just a few hours before the Baron had come storming down from his tower room, shouting that the villain must be arrested.

And before Truefew . . . well, Malkin had not known the one before, but the gooseherd, Pug, who seemed to know not only what was going on in the present but in the past as well, said that before Truefew there had been a Welsh wizard who called himself Gwydion. He had insisted that the Baron's daughter had been transformed into an owl, and that in order to find her, he must have the finest horse, the keenest hawk, the richest clothes, the heaviest purse—for the breaking of spells did not come cheaply—and that he must be free to roam the country far and wide to seek her. Gwydion had lasted quite a long time, Pug had said, grinning; the Welshman had known a trick or two of conjuring, and so he had kept the old Baron dazzled for at least six or seven years. Now it was the time for Mafioso's reign to come to an end. There had been signs for a few weeks now that the Baron was running out of patience, and, rather belatedly, tightening the purse strings. He was lucky that his lands were so fat and rich, for in the last seventeen years, he had squandered more than two-thirds of the immense fortune that had been left to him by his ancestors.

Thump! The noise was close at hand, and Malkin shied a little anxiously and scuttled faster. Under her vast apron, she carried the remains of a cheese pie and a stone bottle of small beer. Her mood changed. It was sad indeed that the old Baron should not even see the treasure and the joy in front of his eyes, spending all his money and his life's blood chasing after unattainable will-o'-the-wisps. His daughter, Margaret, was dead, dead in childbirth seventeen years before, and nothing on Earth or indeed anywhere else would ever bring her back.

Malkin finally reached the mean little room in the remotest part of the castle and pushed open the door. A disconsolate figure sat at the edge of the straw pallet. Malkin hurried in. "Good morning, good morning. The Lord our master is busy, so we can go now if we are very quiet."

"Oh, Malkin . . ." The figure turned and revealed herself to be a girl of about Malkin's age. But in most ways she could be said to be Malkin's opposite. Her skin was golden, like a peach, unlike Malkin's pale cheeks; her hair was as red as a flame, unlike Malkin's coal black bush; her eyes were large, brown, and sorrowful, unlike Malkin's almond-shaped, dancing blue ones; and she was as small and sweetly round as Malkin was tall and fine-boned. But while Malkin was dressed in the stout but serviceable clothes of country folk, this girl's sweet frame, which should have been clothed in the latest London fashions, was clad only in rags and tatters. Malkin would have liked to have given her some of her own things, but the old Baron had ordered that his only grandchild must ever be clad only in rags and tatters, and there were plenty in the castle who delighted in following his orders to the very letter. He had even decreed that she must be called Tattercoats, after her ragged clothes, though her true name was Susanna. It had been her father, Will de Montacour, who had given the name Susanna to her, just days before he had fled his grief and his sadness and vanished to the court of King Henri of France, leaving his baby daughter in the loving care—as he thought—of her grandfather. Every few years de Montacour bethought himself of his daughter, and sent her a rich present and a foolish letter, but never once had he thought to return and see the life his daughter was living.

Malkin sat on the bed and gave Tattercoats the food she had smuggled out. The Baron had decreed a few months before that his granddaughter must not be allowed to leave her miserable room until the evening, and must not be fed till then, but Malkin ignored these cruel orders. If truth be told, she was getting more anxious these days as to the possible fate of Tattercoats. She had heard that an Italian magician known as Oscuro had landed in England, and feared that he might take the place of Mafioso. Oscuro's evil reputation had preceded him. It was thought he was in constant contact with the forces of the night, and certainly he was known to be a poisoner. Pug had said that he had fled Italy just a few steps ahead of justice, which would have executed him as a murderer. "So he comes to England instead," Pug had said, "because in this country we are so dazzled by anything from Italy that even the rankest villain seems like an infinitely subtle mind." Malkin was not sure what Pug meant. She had not met any Italians before, for Mafioso only pretended to be Italian. Everyone knew he was really plain John Browne from the village of Wyre Piddle; everyone, that is, except the Baron. But Pug, who seemed to know things no gooseherd before or since would have even heard of, said that in Italy poison and magic worked together as one.

Thinking of it, Malkin's anxiety made her say sharply to Tattercoats: "Come now, while everyone is busy. Pug is waiting for us."

Tattercoats immediately sprang up, scattering the crumbs of the pie she'd only half eaten. "Oh, Malkin! You are so good to me, you and Pug!"

"Oh, don't talk nonsense," said Malkin, secretly pleased. The fleeting thought crossed her mind that if Tattercoats were treated as she should be, as the Lady Susanna, she would have no time for such as Malkin, and would be more like the Baron, who never seemed to notice his inferiors. Although the Baron's attitude suited Malkin—to be noticed by the Baron seemed a poisoned gift indeed—it wrung her heart to think that her friend Tattercoats might do the same.

Apart from Tattercoats and Pug, Malkin was alone in the world. She had been a foundling. Long ago an old woman had found small Malkin under a bush in her garden, and not for the life of her could she find out who the child belonged to. The old woman had brought Malkin up till she was ten and old enough to find employment as a scullery maid, and then a kitchen maid, in the castle of the Baron of Fisher Forest. Servants never stayed there long because of the Baron's strangeness and the heavy sadness that hung like a stifling black cloud over the castle. But Malkin had nowhere to go, and from the first she had befriended Tattercoats, just as Pug had befriended them both. Occasionally Malkin had thought she remembered flashes of an earlier life, long before she had been found by the old woman, but they remained vague pictures, and she no longer thought about them. She would never find out who her parents were, and it did not matter anymore. She had a name now, a home, food to eat, and friends—that was enough.

» Two «

Malkin and Tattercoats forgot all sadness once they were clear of the gloomy castle. The day was beautiful, clear as glass, the sun's alchemy gilding even the smallest thing with glittering gold. In the meadows beyond the castle, the spring flowers had come out, and the trees were clothed in the softest of green leaves, the grass was silky smooth, and Pug was playing his flute. He had a small wooden reed, whose music was surprisingly sweet and clear and piercing, and they could hear him now, playing a tune that made the spirits soar and the feet fly. They ran to him through the grass and landed laughing in the midst of his dignified flock of geese, who, as always, were clustered around their herder, clucking and honking solemnly in appreciation.

The oldest gander in the flock, who was as dignified as a bishop, honked indignantly at this breach of protocol, but the girls didn't care—they linked hands and danced while Pug played. At last, exhausted, they begged him to stop, and he did, smiling his familiar darting grin. As always Pug was quite transformed by his music. You forgot that he was lame, forgot that his frame was thin, his face pinched and wizened, that his clothes hung on him, that his hair was lank. You only saw his laughing eyes, only heard the bewitching sweetness of his instrument.

Pug accepted the rather mashed remains of the pie with becoming grace, and said, through a mouthful, "Well now, my fine maids, you seem lighthearted indeed today!"

"It is a lovely day," said Tattercoats, rather breathlessly, watching a skylark rising into the clear air. In a moment it would start singing, caroling at the top of its voice, she knew. And so it did, singing and singing like Pug played his flute, singing its heart out, so that tears came to her eyes. "Oh, listen to that!"

They all listened, watching the small bird high up above them, its wings almost still as it poured out its love song to the world, but Malkin and Pug also watched Tattercoats, with her lovely face and her sadness that could go in an instant just with a song. Not for the first time, Malkin's heart was wrung, for there was no hate or anger in Tattercoats, and a constant willingness to be surprised into joy. Foolish, foolish Baron, not to realize that in his granddaughter's heart was a treasure greater than any secret of death, greater than any riches in this world or any other. Pug must have felt the same, for his face was drawn down in the melancholy that was the closest thing to sadness he ever showed. But he said nothing, just watched, and so Malkin was silent too, while the skylark's song went on and on. When it abruptly stopped, Pug said idly, as if the thought had just struck him: "I have heard there is to be a great ball at the court, and that all nobles and their families are to be invited. They are to be presented to the Queen and much more besides. A messenger is riding at this very moment toward the castle to tell the Baron."

Malkin glanced sharply at him. How did he know? But Pug's eyes—green as grass, green as the forest leaves—did not waver. Tattercoats, missing the exchange of glances, said, *"Ohhh . . . I wish . . ."* on a long, drawn out sigh.

Malkin knew what she was thinking. The poor, foolish girl, despite the Baron's prohibitions, had a head full of sweet fancies, and no doubt imagined herself at the ball, her grandfather's heart quite melted. She did not have the heart to disenchant the girl, but in any case Pug got there before her.

"What is it you wish, Tattercoats, my dear?" he said, as if he were truly obtuse.

Tattercoats looked at him a little suspiciously. She might be innocent, but she was not simple. She said, a little huffily, "You do not need to tell me it is impossible, Pug, but I can still wish, can't I?"

Pug grinned. "Of course you can," he agreed. "But it is *not* impossible, Tattercoats, my dear."

I wish he wouldn't speak as if he were an impossibly old man, Malkin thought crossly. She was not sure quite how old Pug was; some days he seemed ancient, others as young as a child, but he was surely only about twenty years old in reality.

"Pug," she said sternly, "you must not play games like this; it is not fair or just."

"Game? What game?" Pug was quite solemn now. He lifted his flute to his lips and played two or three notes. "I was never so serious in all my life."

"But what . . ." And then Malkin broke off, staring at a strange procession winding its way to the castle on the road just below them. There was a tall man dressed in the height of the most outrageous fashion, a vast stiff ruff around his neck, setting off his teased, curled, waist-length silver blond hair. He sat stiffly on a massive horse, his brocade doublet nipped at the waist, his silken hose so large that he appeared to have segmented legs. He wore a short, winged, triangular cloak of great splendor, and on his head was a kind of large velvet bonnet. In fact, his entire appearance suggested some gigantic insect—a bee perhaps, or a wasp. Behind this singular personage rode two or three others, much more plainly dressed, who were obviously his retainers.

The watchers in the meadows drew in their breaths. "Well," said Tattercoats, her eyes shining, "that must be the Queen's messenger. Oh!" And she clasped her hands together.

"Mmmm," murmured Pug thoughtfully and noncommittally, while Malkin stared at the apparition below them, the laughter bubbling up within her.

"Malkin," said Tattercoats, jumping to her feet, "we must return to the castle, because I want to be there when the messenger issues his invitation."

"Wait, wait," said Pug, whose eyes were still on the road. Malkin followed his glance and saw a dust cloud some ways in the distance, behind the splendid procession. The dust cloud swiftly resolved itself into a russet-clad man with long autumn brown hair streaming out behind him, riding fast on a slender brown horse in the direction of the castle. She looked swiftly at Pug, suddenly remembering the Italian magician Oscuro. "Yes," she said to Tattercoats, "you are right, we must return." Her heart beat uncomfortably hard.

As they left the meadow and headed back toward the castle by the familiar hidden ways, Malkin turned back once and saw Pug standing perfectly still in the midst of his ruffled geese, his eyes on the road. And a slow, cold feeling crept over her at the intensity of his gaze and the stillness of his body.

» Three «

It just went to show that appearances must not be taken as the substance, Malkin thought as she peered from behind the door at the extraordinary sight in the great hall. For the autumnal man on his brown horse was not Oscuro at all, but the Queen's messenger, and the splendid insect was the Italian magician himself.

Malkin's heart was easier as she looked at the ridiculous figure that Oscuro presented; no one as foppish, as overblown as this could possibly be any danger at all. Look at him, the knave, she thought, cramming a fist into her mouth to stop herself from laughing out loud. What a figure he cuts! Fluttering-fingered, teasing-voiced, gold-buttoned, smooth-tongued: if this were the best Italian magic could offer, why, it was a shame indeed! Oscuro had a high, thin, fluting voice, and he talked and talked and talked, while the Baron looked bewildered—as well he might, the fool. Here was another candidate to empty his purse.

Then Malkin, in the midst of her smug contempt, suddenly saw the magician's eyes narrowing, saw his hard violet gaze, and knew that evil came in many guises. To expect it to come dark-robed, deep-voiced, and seemingly not of this world was to make a grave mistake. She shrank back in the shadow of the door, the magician's gaze burning into her soul. He had not seen her, had he? Surely not. In any case, even if he had, it would not matter, for a mere serving maid would be of no concern to one as grand as he. Oh, Baron of Fisher Forest, she thought as she hurried back up the corridors to tell Tattercoats what she had seen, this time you have bitten off more than your teeth can manage!

But Tattercoats did not seem in the least interested in Oscuro or the danger he might represent. "Malkin, Malkin," she burst out as soon as the other girl came through the door. "Tell me, what did he say? Oh, what did he say?"

She did not mean Oscuro; she did not give a fig for Oscuro. Malkin sighed. "There is to be a ball at the court, in honor of the birthday of the Queen's godson, the Earl of Malmsey. And all the nobles—and their families—are expected to attend. For all, he said, are under the protection of the Queen."

"He said that? Under the Queen's protection? All their families?" breathed Tattercoats. "Oh, what did my grandfather say?"

"He nodded and bowed, and thanked the messenger . . . and then . . ."

"And then?" Tattercoats echoed eagerly.

"The messenger left. He was in a hurry. He had still more people to see."

"Oh!" Tattercoats clasped her hands together. "You see, Malkin, you see. This means I can go. I must go, indeed, for the Queen wishes it so."

Malkin looked at her. She could not bear to tell her the rest of what she had heard. For when the messenger had gone, the silken Oscuro, who had been listening in silence, said softly, "But Lord, this surely cannot apply to you, for you have—forgive me—no family, have you?" And the Baron had looked at him for a moment with anger in his eyes, so that the magician had taken an elegant step back. Then he had sighed and said: "Signor Oscuro, you little know the trials of my life. Sad, bereft, lonely . . . so much pain and grief on my mind. . . ."

She did not tell all this to Tattercoats, for what need was there to hurt her by reporting her grandfather's selfish words? Tattercoats talked excitedly of the ball for a while, sure her grandfather would let her go because, after all, the Queen had decreed it so. Malkin did not have the heart to tell her that the Queen could have no knowledge of her existence and therefore could not protect her in any way. Soon Malkin excused herself and, leaving the other girl to her dreams, slipped out of the castle again and ran down the meadows to find Pug. She would not dare stay long, for preparations for the evening meal would soon begin and she would be missed.

While Pug listened in silence, Malkin told him everything. His geese were grazing peacefully in the meadow, the oldest gander pacing up and down with his waddling gait, but they were a little disturbed by Malkin's coming. Pug played a few notes on his flute and they were quite still. Finally, when she had finished, he merely said, "So."

"So! So!" Malkin exclaimed exasperatedly. "What are we to do, Pug? Our sweet girl believes she is under the protection of the Queen, of the Queen's own country, and that will never . . ."

"She is under the protection of the Other Country," said Pug, and his words were so sudden, so unexpected, that Malkin could only stare. An echo of something rang in her mind, but try as she might, she could not capture it. She frowned and then shrugged. "You speak in riddles, Pug, when grave things are being decided. She wants to go to the ball, and she cannot, can she? The magician may well cause her harm, and she does not even know it. It worries me, Pug, and all you can do is riddle!"

"Ah, what is the good of worrying?" said Pug, smiling. "She *will* go to the ball, because that is the way it must be. Whether that brings her any good is another thing, for it may end by bringing her ill. As to the magician . . ." he shrugged in his turn. "You believed a night-magician should look like the night, not bold and flashy as the day. Now you see it is not so; perhaps you might also see that all his famed might is nothing more than rumor and idle gossip. That is the way of this world, that things of air, rumors, should have more substance than things of the earth."

Malkin retorted: "You have not seen him, and I have. He may look like a water fly, but by heaven, Pug, he is not! Rather is he like a forked snake or a spitting toad, and his finery is but glamour. You know that real wizards can indeed cast glamour and make everything seem as it is not. . . ." She frowned and shook her head. As she said the words, a quicksilver memory leaped into her mind: a vague picture of a thin, bright face, smiling secretively. Almost as soon as it had come into her mind, though, it vanished.

She looked at Pug, and saw that he was watching her carefully. For a moment she felt as if he knew what had been in her mind. Then the feeling vanished like the memory when he said: "Malkin, Malkin, you should stop listening to every small bat-whisper, every goodwife's tale. The important thing is that our Susanna, our Tattercoats, should go to the ball."

"How can she even do that?" said Malkin, distracted. "She has no clothes to wear."

"There is a chest," observed Pug, "hidden under the roots of the elder tree near the dairy. Dig there tonight and you will come to it. Bring it to me. Then tomorrow come here with her and we will see what we will see."

Malkin stared at him. "How do you know this?" Her skin prickled with unease. But he grinned at her with his familiar mischief and said, "Oh, I listen to every bat-whisper and every goodwife's tale!" And with that, at least for the moment, she had to be satisfied.

≫ ≫ ≪ ≪

Malkin served that night at dinner, the grandest feast the castle had seen for some time. There was beef and pork and mutton and rabbit, roasted and stuffed; trussed poultry of all kinds; whitings and oysters and wildfowl; sugared strawberries and cherries and apricots and dewberries piled high on plates; and plates and plates of sweet comfits of all sorts. There was gilt gingerbread and marzipan and rosewater sugarplate; the candied root of sea-holly and sugared violets; all kinds of wines, from sack sweetened with spices and sugar through Rhenish wine and the best Gascon claret, right down to the strong beers favored by city people, known in those parts as Dragon's Milk and Mad Dog. And Mad Dog is what they'll be, aye, and bitten hard by the dragon, Malkin thought sourly as she fetched and carried plates.

For the occasion, to celebrate his renewal of hope in a new enterprise, the Baron had invited not only his new guests but also Mafioso and all the workmen, and he presided over this rather doubtful gathering, his wasted face glowing fitfully from the false fellowship of the wine. He had also, much to Malkin's amazement, cut his long beard, trimming it to just under his chin so that now he looked less like Old Father Frost and a little more like the serious nobleman he should have been. As to Oscuro, he had sat quietly at the table listening to and watching the others. But Malkin had been uncomfortably aware of his violet gaze resting on her, thoughtfully, now and again. No more, really, she told herself, than he watched the others, but somehow she distrusted this quietness more than his earlier garrulity.

At last, at long, long last, the last toast had been drunk, the last song roared out. Oscuro, whom Malkin noticed had hardly drunk at all, had long since retired to the chamber prepared for him, and as for the Baron, he had long since gone up to his tower room to spend what remained of the night in more fruitless redeye book wanderings. Or perhaps tonight to sleep, for now Oscuro was here. . . .

Mafioso and his henchmen lay snoring amid the plates as the servants tried to clear up (although in the morning he would somehow vanish with a cartload of fine and precious things: ebony and rosewood and Venetian glass goblets and many such things). Finally everything was done, and the servants retired for the last few hours of gray night.

When she was sure all was quiet, Malkin slipped out of the castle and scurried toward the outbuildings. The moon was up, and it was quite light. She carried a spade filched from the gardens. When she reached the elder tree, she looked around her. Perfect silence. Quickly, wasting no time, she began to dig, the earth flying around her. Soon she heard a dull thud as the spade hit something. She dug more quickly, and in no time uncovered the lid of a small wooden chest with metal clasps. Surprisingly, considering the chest's look of great age, the clasps were still shiny.

She lifted the chest out and, without stopping, filled in the hole and patted the earth down as well as she could. It would be unlikely that the disturbance in the ground would be noticed, as the elder tree was out of sight behind the dairy.

The chest was surprisingly light, as if it contained nothing but feathers, and her heart sank within her as she thought that

Pug might have been playing an elaborate trick on her. She tried to push at the clasps, but they held fast.

She trudged down to the mean little hut where Pug always slept, surrounded by his charges, guarding them from foxes. He was squatting on his haunches outside the hut, perfectly still, and for a moment he appeared not to see her. Then he turned and grinned. "Ah, you have it, then!"

"Yes," said Malkin shortly, putting the chest down. "I hope it is wha . . ." But she did not finish her sour little sentence, for Pug had opened the chest. She had not even noticed him touching the clasps, yet here was the chest, open to the moonlight. All questions died in her mind, for there, shimmering in the chest, was the most beautiful dress she had ever seen, in a fabric she couldn't even identify.

"Feathers, it's made of," Pug said softly. "A feather from every bird in the world. They gave one each, gladly."

The dress shimmered with a thousand slivers and arrows of blue and gray and red and black, a million soft, shining downs. It was as light to the touch as if it hardly existed at all. Dove, kingfisher, parrot, pheasant, woodcock, hawk, eagle, skylark—all the thousands upon thousands of birds in the world had each given a feather, Pug said. Malkin looked at it in wonder and a tiny griping of the heart that she would never wear anything as beautiful as this. Then the thought vanished as she thought of Tattercoats's face when she saw the dress, and of it floating around her soft, round body.

"She will look like a princess," she said softly. "Our sweet girl, Pug—she'll be the magnet for all eyes at Queen Elizabeth's court."

"Yes," said Pug. His curious gaze was on Malkin, and she flushed a little under it, but held it steadily. "This is truly a dress for a princess."

No, she would *not* be jealous! "What will she wear on her feet, Pug?"

As an answer, Pug simply gathered up the dress, so light and soft it hardly took up any space in his arms. Under it were a pair of shimmering green slippers and a small cap of deep green velvet and lace.

Malkin picked them up. The shoes felt like no other she had ever touched. They were not stiff and hard, as the gentry's shoes usually were. No, these were soft—not the softness of feathers, but rather the softness of the grass in the meadows. She looked up at Pug, who nodded. "The grasses of the meadows and the flowers," he said, and now Malkin could see that there were indeed, within the shimmering green, tiny points of red and blue and yellow and violet, like miniature flowers.

"And the hat, made of the velvet moss of the woods," she whispered, the words coming unbidden from somewhere deep inside her. "And the lace, of the streams."

"As you can see," said Pug, with a curiously satisfied smile. And he put his flute to his lips and began to play a soft tune. But Malkin hardly heard him, lost in wonder at the beautiful, fragile things laid out in the moonlight in front of her. She could hardly wait for morning, so she could show Tattercoats.

» Four «

Malkin's dreams were jagged and disordered that short, light night. In her dreams she was not sure if she was excited or afraid, or maybe both. When she woke, feeling unrefreshed and gritty-eyed, she lay for a moment on her straw pallet without moving. Pug seemed to be quite sure that the impossible could indeed be achieved, and that he, Malkin, and Tattercoats would somehow leave Fisher Forest, travel to London, and go to the ball. But how? In the cold, gray light of dawn, the whole enterprise seemed more impossible than ever. She remembered the feather dress and the shoes and the cap, and rubbed at her eyes. Perhaps that had been a part of her dream. She had dreamt it all: digging under the elder tree, the chest, and Pug's calm words. She was no longer sure. She struggled up, pulled on her clothes over her shift, put on her shoes, tied on her cap. She threw some water over her face from the bowl that was kept on the table just outside. The shock of the water woke her properly, but her head still felt thick.

She dragged herself around for much of the morning, so that once or twice she was spoken to very sharply by the cook, and even had her ears boxed. She should go and see Tattercoats and bring her out to Pug, she thought vaguely, but somehow she felt reluctant. Everything felt like it was too much trouble, too difficult. And an insistent little voice reminded her that she would never wear a beautiful dress and go to the ball, that Tattercoats would forget her once she was the Lady Susanna, that all she had to look forward to was growing old in the service of the Baron. And if she went to see Tattercoats now and brought her out to Pug, the die would be cast, there would be no turning back. So it was better not to go at all. Things would stay as they were: not so good for Tattercoats, it must be admitted, but she still had Malkin and Pug as friends, she still had her sweet nature, she was in a place she knew. Imagine her at the court, she who had never been taught to curtsy or to talk prettily or to act like a fluttery girl in front of men! Why, it would be an unkindness to take her out of this place and expose her to the humiliations that attended all provincials in the big city. And besides, it would not make the Baron love her. He would be furious if he found out what they were planning. He would likely dismiss both Malkin and Pug, and they'd be wandering the roads, starving, and unable to protect Tattercoats any longer.

So the day passed in not very happy fashion. There was a good deal of activity in the kitchen because of the guests and the impending trip of the Baron to London. The gossip in the kitchen was that the Italian would be going with him; he was certainly a fine enough gentleman to be at the court. One of the grander servants relaxed sufficiently to say that the Italian was a Count in his own country, with a name as long as your arm, but that his modesty precluded him from using it in the course of his professional life as astrologer and magician. One of the cooks let it be known that when his brother had been in the army, serving in various places, he had come across people just like that: extraordinary, they were. To a man and a woman, the servants appeared to approve of Oscuro, which was odd, in a way, because the man's appearance was not calculated to win disciples among the ordinary people. Malkin had glimpsed him that day, discoursing in a lordly fashion with the Baron, dressed in flame-colored taffeta from head to foot, the crystal buttons on his doublet shaped like miniature suns, his hose of silk, and his cross-garters a lurid shade of yellow. Normally such dress would have had the cooks mincing in ribald parody and the maids giggling helplessly. Malkin had seen it happen before. Also extraordinary was that Oscuro appeared hail-fellow-well-met to the men and smoldering-elegant to the women. Malkin herself could not quite work it out—her head was too heavy. She found she had no feeling for Oscuro, good or bad. Her fear of him yesterday seemed like a distant dream too—like the feather dress.

Just as the sun was sinking in the West, Malkin was sent outside by the chief cook to ask the gardeners for some herbs. She walked down the path toward the gardens, around the garden walls, and through the gate. She could not see anyone there at first; then, at a distance, hoeing between two rows of vegetables, she glimpsed a gardener. She hurried toward him because the cook had enjoined her to be quick; his stews needed just that last touch of thyme and rosemary.

"Good man," she called out as she came near, "will you gather some herbs for the kitchens. I am pressed for time; the cook is waiting."

The gardener muttered something, but Malkin paid no attention. Gardeners were always as soreheaded as bears; they believed that indoor servants had an easy time of it and that gardeners worked much harder. She gazed out over the garden rather impatiently, waiting. In the West the sun was almost on the horizon, its distant fires clothing the hill, the time neither night nor day, and all at once she felt uneasy.

"Is it thyme you want," she suddenly heard the gardener say, "or rosemary—rosemary for remembrance?" The voice startled her with its familiarity, and she looked at him more closely. The eyes he lifted to her were familiar: bright, darting eyes, green as grass, green as the forest leaves. How had she not seen? "Pug!" she cried. Guilt seized her then. "Oh, Pug, I'm sorry. I've failed. I did not bring Tattercoats to you."

He did not reassure her, but simply said, "Fetch Tattercoats now."

"But the cook . . ."

"I will take the herbs. I know cooks. They are fierce," he said, grinning. "Go. I will be in the meadow when you return."

She did not ask any questions, merely raced up the path toward the buildings. Taking a deep breath, she scurried down the corridors toward Tattercoats's room. As her steps took her closer to Tattercoats's quarters and further from the outside, she was aware of the reluctance coming back, and of a dozen questions crowding into her head. How had she not seen it was Pug till he spoke? How had Pug known she would come outside? He had not seemed surprised or angered by her failure to bring Tattercoats out earlier, which meant he must have known what would happen. And why was she so reluctant now? A real fear iced her spine, but she forced herself to ignore it until she reached Tattercoats's room.

The girl was standing at her small window, and staring out through the open wooden shutters. She did not even have any glass in her window; the general, Mafioso-led improvements to the castle had not touched her room—and never would now that the builder had gone. Perfectly still, she was watching the last of the sunset over the hills. Her stillness, the way her form was outlined against the dying light, made her seem almost a stranger, some foreign princess fallen on hard times. Malkin drew in a breath, and then Tattercoats turned. "Good evening," she said in her low, sweet voice, without a hint of reproach. "It is good to see you, Malkin."

Tears sprang into Malkin's eyes, but she blinked them away sharply. "You must come with me," she said. "It is important, Pug says."

"But Malkin, you know it is nearly night, and I am never allowed out at night. Things are abroad that might hurt me, they told me."

Malkin snorted, glad to have a way to express the anger she felt against the Baron, against callousness, against even her own self. "They tell you anything," she said tightly. "You will be safe. You are in the protection of the Other Country."

The words had slipped out as naturally as a song, and she wondered what the other girl would think, but Tattercoats only nodded, as if she understood. Malkin felt humbled by her acceptance.

"We must go, then, Malkin," Tattercoats said, as if it were her own idea now. She *could* be infuriating, Malkin thought, losing her awe. She was like a child. Malkin felt like an old woman beside her.

» Five «

Dusk was a strange time to be abroad, despite Malkin's brave words, and without speaking of it, the two girls hurried. At the crossroads between night and day, dusk harbored all kinds of shadows and fancies that in bright day could be explained away and in night would be cloaked in absolute danger. Despite this, however, Malkin felt clearheaded and strong. She remembered Pug's words of the previous day about Oscuro, and thought that perhaps the day could hide as much infamy, or more, as the night. Pug did not seem afraid of the night, despite the fact that as a gooseherd he had perhaps more reason to be so than Malkin, for it was at night that the foxes and wolves came out, just as the human foxes and wolves did. But then he knew the foxes and the wolves, both animal and human. They were not shadows slipping in and out of day for him, they were realities of the night.

They arrived quickly at Pug's hut, but the gooseherd was nowhere to be seen. Tattercoats was plainly nervous.

Tattercoats whispered, "Malkin, can't we go inside and wait for him?"

Inside would be dim and full of the smell of sleep and feathers and goose manure: good, warm smells that comforted and reassured. Outside, under the great bowl of the sky, was a freedom without limits that could be terrifying. The thoughts flashed through Malkin's mind before she could really understand them, but she said softly: "Yes, why not? I am sure Pug will not be long. Perhaps the cook has detained him. If he spoke to the under-cook, then we may wait here a long while, for that one can talk the hind and front legs off a mule, indeed."

Tattercoats nodded and yawned. "Let us go in, then, dear Malkin." And Malkin was absurdly pleased by the endearment.

The hut was as dim and warm and strong-smelling as Malkin had expected. You could only just see the pale glow of the geese's white down in the semidarkness. As the girls entered, the birds rustled a little, disturbed, but soon settled down, their heads back under their wings. The girls crept to the corner where Pug had his few belongings and stretched out on the bundles of soft, clean-smelling straw he had spread out. In the dimness Malkin could not see her friend's face properly, but she heard her sigh, and the soft words, "Oh, Malkin, if only heart-wishes would come true!"

"You will go to the ball. You know that," said Malkin.

Tattercoats was silent a moment. "It is not that I was thinking of," she said, but just what she had been thinking of, Malkin did not discover, for at that moment Pug came in, silently pushing the door. His geese did not stir at all as he came in on soft feet, and he did not seem at all surprised to see the girls there. He sat at the edge of the straw, his lame leg held out stiffly in front of him.

"I brought these for you," he said, passing out savory crumbs of some pie crust or other. They ate in silence for a moment, then he observed: "It would be best if you stayed here tonight, Tattercoats. They will not think of looking here, and we will leave before first light. I would like to leave earlier, but I know people do not like the night roads."

Both girls turned to him in amazement. Malkin, her pulse hammering in her throat, said, "What do you mean . . . Are you . . ."

"It is just as I thought. Oscuro has wasted no time. It is fortunate that you brought Tattercoats when you did, Malkin. There was precious little time left." He made no reproach, but Malkin felt the fear of what he said like a chill wind. She made no reply, but Tattercoats got up. Her voice trembling, she whispered: "Pug, you are just trying to frighten me. I won't let you! Where would I go? And why?"

"You want to go to London, to the court, to the ball, do you not, my Lady?" he said, still seated. Even in the dimness, Malkin could see his grin.

"Yes, but . . . Pug, do not mock me! How can I go when I have no clothes? And anyway I must get my grandfather's consent, and . . ."

"The chest is over there," Pug said without replying directly. "Malkin, would you bring it here?"

Malkin looked at him for a moment more before going silently over to get the chest. Despite the confusion in her mind, something else was growing, something that was starting to build a picture of echoes and wisps of memory and understanding.

Tattercoats looked from one to the other of them, her smooth, peachy face filled with uncertainty. She had to be prodded to open the chest, and when she did, she stared in without a word.

"Well?" Malkin said at last. "Well, do you like it?"

In the semidarkness of the hut, the feather dress glowed with a soft light. Malkin felt such a yearning to touch it, pull it out, that it was almost like a physical pain. But Tattercoats was still silent, looking into the chest with a strange look on her face.

"Try it on," said Malkin, the words scalding her throat with her own longing. "Over your clothes," she said impatiently, interpreting Tattercoats's unease. Pug watched them both. He was not moving or speaking, but Malkin was sure he was still grinning.

At last the girl spoke. "You are right, it is beautiful indeed . . . but . . ."

"But?" Malkin was startled, and angry.

"I have seen such dresses in old pictures of my ancestors, at the castle," said Tattercoats, speaking fast. "But they are not . . . not the fashion of these days." Her head was bent. "And at court . . . at court they will know that."

Malkin could only stare. Fashion! Old pictures! This was a dress unique, magnificent, never before seen.

As no one spoke, Tattercoats warmed to her theme. "These days ladies wear silk and taffeta all stiff and shiny. They look like comfits, yes, and their caps are brilliant with jewels. Yes, sometimes I've looked out of the window, and I have seen them. . . . These colors are pretty, but they are old. . . ." She looked beseechingly toward them. "The material is thin, not thick; soft, not stiff. I don't even know what it is; I can't even name it. The colors should be brighter, and . . ."

"Are you out of your mind?" Malkin moved toward the girl and dropped to her knees beside the chest. The feather dress lay there in all its beauty. She touched it gently. "There never has been anything so beautiful." Tears sprang to her eyes. "In this you will be more beautiful than the most beautiful lady at the court. Won't she, Pug?"

Pug had also got to his feet. He was standing beside them, and now that he was so close, Malkin could see that his face was lit by a darting smile.

"We will have to find something more to your taste, then," he said. "But that can wait. For the moment you must rest." He saw Malkin's rebellious glance and held a finger to his lips. "Malkin, you must return to the castle, for if they miss you too, there will be no end of trouble. But come back here at the first cockcrow, and then we will go."

Malkin slowly closed the chest. She was still stunned by Tattercoats's reaction. It was obvious that the girl had not seen what was in front of her, but something quite different, some muddled picture in her mind. But she had no chance to question any further, for Pug gently but firmly pushed her outside. "Let you sleep, and our sweet girl too," he said when they were outside the door. "The morning will bring new counsel."

Malkin waited to hear more, but the gooseherd had turned decisively on his heel and walked back into the hut, shutting the door behind him.

» Six «

"Hemlock and henbane!" Malkin cursed under her breath as she stumbled back up the path toward the castle. If you had asked her why she was cursing, she would have said that it was because she was annoyed. Annoyed because of Tattercoats's reaction to the dress, annoyed because she herself did not really understand what was going on. Annoyance, that's all, she would have said firmly. But there was no cursing away the longing, the questions, the beginnings of memory's return; no cursing away the pulse of unease and excitement that beat under her skin.

As she reached the castle and slipped into the servants' quarters, her heart hammered loudly within her. There were lights, noise, unaccustomed activity for this time of night. In the hubbub Malkin's arrival was not noticed, except by one of the other maids who said to her, with a sour look: "You're never here when there is work to be done. Where were you? We were . . ."

Malkin grinned at her, shrugged, and escaped down the corridors. But they were full of swirling groups of servants, talking excitedly in groups, so she stopped and listened. What she heard made her heart race.

"I tell you, they can't find her!" snapped one of the maids to an underling. "You'd think the foolish girl would make things easy for people for once in her life!"

"But the Baron had never shown much interest in her," ventured the underling.

And the maid snapped back: "Well, he's changed his mind, hasn't he? It's that Italian. He has persuaded the Baron that Tattercoats should go to the ball. Apparently he knows something important, has got some plan or other. Don't ask me what it is!

The fact is, she can't be found. And we've all been promised a bonus if we can find her and turn her into a sight fit for the court. Drat the girl! Can't she be more considerate?"

In her corner Malkin clenched her fists. At all other times, the servants paid poor Tattercoats absolutely no attention at all; indeed, had it not been for Malkin, they would probably have forgotten even to feed her. But now they were all speaking animatedly of her. Malkin heard that under Oscuro's instructions, men had been sent out on search parties, that the Baron was pacing his hall, talking loudly to the magician. Malkin was bewildered and disturbed. What did it mean? If the Baron had had a change of heart and Oscuro had persuaded him to this, then why had Pug declared that there was danger? Why had he said Tattercoats must be kept away? It made no sense—unless Oscuro's motives were not what they appeared to be. Or even Pug's. . . . No, surely not. And why was the Baron agreeing when he had surely engaged Oscuro on this fool's errand of bringing his dead daughter back to life? Nothing quite made sense. Malkin cursed under her breath again.

Making a sudden decision, Malkin slipped away into the kitchen, where she snatched up a tray laden with comfits and walked confidently toward the hall. Nobody challenged her. Lights blazed in the hall too, and the door was slightly open. She moved to the door and looked in. There was the Baron, pacing indeed, as the servants had said, and in a corner, at ease in a chair, the Italian. Oscuro appeared to have his eyes closed, but the Baron kept talking and pacing, pacing and talking, up and down the polished tile floor with its geometric patterns, round and round the hall with its brand-new gold and silver wall cloths covered in scenes of hunting and jousting and classical mythology—all the newfangled stuff that Mafioso had ordered to replace the dusty, ancient tapestries. Round and round, up and down he walked, and as he walked, he said: "I always thought . . . I always thought there was more to it than met the eye. And now. I can wait no more, and of course she will be found! Do you say, are you sure my Margaret is a prisoner in that perilous realm?" He stopped and looked at Oscuro, who opened his eyes wearily.

Malkin shrank back. The Italian yawned and rubbed at his eyes. He said, "You know that if a human tithe is paid to our friends, the People of Peace, they will free their prisoners."

"Is that so? But can we be sure they will do this? Can we be sure they will keep their word?" the Baron cried.

Oscuro looked at him. "Sure? You do not think I can do this? You do not believe me, perhaps?" he asked silkily.

Malkin saw the Baron flinch at the other man's tone. She waited for the explosion that did not come. Instead, the Baron said humbly: "I am sorry, Oscuro. I will do as you say. If my grand-daughter cannot be found by others, we must find her."

"We will," said Oscuro. "Never fear. If not here, why then . . . all young girls love balls, my Lord."

"Yes, yes," said the Baron impatiently. "I daresay. And you think that if the tithe . . ."

Oscuro yawned again. "Yes, my Lord," he said curtly. "The People of Peace keep their word."

"It is indeed wonderful," said the Baron, ignoring the yawn and the tone, "that you should have come to me! Now at last, at last, I will see my Margaret again!"

In the corridor Malkin felt frozen to the spot, her head spinning with the implications of what she had heard. Somehow Oscuro seemed to have persuaded the Baron that his dear Margaret was not dead but enchanted, kept spellbound by the spells of the People of Peace. That was one of their names: they were also known as the Good Neighbors, and the Friends, for you did not speak their real name, which was *fairy*. Some people said they did not exist at all, others that they were behind every strange event, every inexplicable happening. Kidnappings; the wasting away of perfectly healthy people; the thievery of all kinds of things; the sinister transformations of illness, of craziness, of grief; the disappearances of family men, of pretty girls; the sudden deaths of children; even unexplained bruises on milkmaids' ankles—all were spoken of as the work of the Friends, the People of Peace. And kinder things too: the doubling of cream in a cow's milk, the floors clean-swept in the mornings, the luck of an innocent, the spell of good music, the golden words of a poet. Their land, which lay both beside that of mortals and within it, was the perilous realm, a place of enchantment and danger. They were immortals, who nevertheless would one day pass away, at the end of the world. It was said by some that they had once been rebel angels who had followed Lucifer's banner at first, but then had thought better of it, and begged for God's forgiveness. This had been given, but they'd still had to serve out a kind of penance, which was that they could not live in heaven anymore. So now they lived in the Otherland, the fairy realm, and in part it was their sadness at being exiled from heaven that made them so unpredictable and dangerous and quick to anger. Yet they were not evil, not demons at all. And so Oscuro must have divined, or pretended to, that Margaret was not dead but spell-bound as their prisoner. It was a clever thing to suggest if you wanted to wind the Baron around your little finger, for there had been many other stories of young women spirited away by the People of Peace, with lifeless bodies left in their place to be buried by grieving relatives who truly thought they had died, or perhaps rescued from enthrallment by one who might take their place—willingly or unwillingly. Malkin had never heard of human tithes being given to them, but certainly there had been strange stories of people disappearing into the fairy realm. Of course, it might all be nonsense, just another unscrupulous charlatan's words. As Pug had said, the Baron had been convinced of enchantment once before, when Gwydion the Welsh wizard had held sway. It had always been at the back of his mind.

Yet the Baron seemed to believe it was true; worse, he seemed to be prepared to sacrifice his own granddaughter. Even worse, there was something about Oscuro which troubled Malkin greatly; she did not think he was altogether a charlatan, as so many of the others had been. The horror of what the Baron proposed to do chilled Malkin to the bone, and she was about to run away to warn Tattercoats and Pug at once when the Baron, suddenly catching sight of her, came to the door. "What do you want?" he said, and Malkin, in the midst of her fear, could only point at her tray and stammer, "Comfits, Sir."

He waved an impatient hand. "Bring them in then, girl. Don't skulk around outside. The comfits won't walk in by themselves." He did not even look at her properly, but she was uncomfortably aware that Oscuro was watching her.

At close quarters the magician was even more handsome than he appeared at a distance, though not quite as young; fine wrinkles cobwebbed the corners of his eyes, and the skin of his neck was not as smooth as it might once have been. He was closer to thirty now than to twenty, Malkin thought. But these imperfections somehow only added to his beauty, a beauty that would have been too coldly perfect otherwise. He smiled—a thin smile, but a smile nevertheless—and his strange violet eyes as they rested on Malkin did not seem suspicious or hostile but rather, appraising, in a way that made her color slightly.

"Thank you," he said softly. "I am very fond of comfits."

This time his smile was warm, and to her dismay, Malkin felt herself warmed all over by it. He held her eyes for a moment, and the oddest feeling stole over her, a yearning in her belly, a flutter in her throat, a griping in her chest. She dropped her eyes, made a curtsy, and said woodenly, "Good night, Sir."

The Baron did not even notice her departure. He was still pacing and muttering to himself, and Malkin thought for the first time that he was perhaps quite mad. But the thought was idle, without urgency. The warmth of Oscuro's charm, like a golden bubble, stayed with her as she walked slowly away. A man like this could not possibly be bad. If he had persuaded the Baron his daughter was enchanted by the People of Peace, there could be no harm come of it. Either they did not exist, in which case it did not matter, or they did, in which case his wiliness was presumably a good match for theirs. And he had apparently also persuaded the Baron that his granddaughter must be brought into the world. Italians were subtle, clever; it was entirely possible that Oscuro had understood that the old man's grief had become a kind of craziness, and he was at present playing two different games to solve the situation—most likely to his own advantage, but not necessarily to Tattercoats's detriment. The golden bubble shimmered around her, and she was about to turn back and tell them where Tattercoats was when all at once she heard the unmistakable sound of Pug's pipe, floating in on the air. The notes were sweet as ever, but there was a strange urgency to them that made her palms feel sweaty.

The bubble burst. Instead, Malkin felt such a sense of fear that she was sure the others would smell its sour rankness. She hurried down the corridors, trying unsuccessfully to outdistance the sweet, insistent sounds, until she reached her own chamber. Trembling, she flung herself on the bed. She was not sure of anything anymore, but she knew she must go at first cockcrow and be with Tattercoats, no matter what happened. She thought she would stay awake till then, her head whirling with thoughts and terrors, but was asleep before she knew it.

It was not first cockcrow when she awoke, but somewhat later. The sky was very dark, still, the kind of opaque darkness, total darkness, that comes not long before the dawn. Malkin dressed hurriedly and, reaching under her mattress, took the few coins she had been able to save from her employment. She folded her one handkerchief, her comb, and one good ribbon and put all these things into the battered waist-purse someone had once given her. She tied it carefully on her waist, pushed her hair into her cap, scrubbed at her gritty eyes, pulled on her shoes, and was gone. On her way out of the castle, she stopped quickly at the kitchen and took a knife that would not be missed too soon. She put the knife carefully inside the folds of her bodice, her mouth uncomfortably dry at the implications of what she was doing. Thievery of any kind was severely punished. Now, going from her safe employment, she was turning herself into one of those "rogues, vagabonds, and sturdy beggars" the law was so hard on. She had seen a few of those kinds of people pass by the castle gates and had never thought she would become one of them. But . . . she would not *think* now, she would merely do.

» Seven «

Pug made no comment on her lateness as she, puffing slightly, arrived at his hut. He was squatting by his prepared pack carving a stick as she approached, and he looked up with a quick grin. Tattercoats was beside him, huddled into her ragged cloak. Despite the fact that it was June, the early morning was not warm. Tattercoats's eyes—her sweet, guileless eyes—were on her, full of weariness. But then she smiled a wan smile, and the sight gave Malkin renewed heart. Well, so she would be a vagabond or a sturdy beggar or any other of those names, but at least she would be with her friends. On the high roads they would wander, would see the world that lay beyond the frontiers of the woods that had bounded their lives till then. They would go to London, would, perhaps, see the Queen. Yes, that would be wonderful indeed. She closed her mind's eye to the other things that could happen, to the potholed, dangerous roads, the moors infested with High Lawyers—or the "gentlemen of the road," as people called them—who robbed rich and poor alike with gay abandon, or the cozeners who gulled victims into willingly handing over their money. In the city, poor country folk such as they would be an easy target. Worse still were the constables who hauled in not the experienced, wily criminals, but the poor fools and innocents who had only lately taken to wandering. These were only some of the dangers, but she refused, in this moment of strange freedom, to consider them. Even more, because she was ashamed, did she refuse to think of that strange moment at the castle, Oscuro's eyes on her, and her own reaction. She said, rather roughly: "Let us go, then. Why are we waiting? The castle is already in an uproar. It will not be long before they expand their searches further afield." Why, indeed, had they not come here already? She would not ask, though she wondered.

"Now," Pug said, getting up. He went back into the hut, but not before Malkin saw that the stick had been carved into a crude but strangely lifelike representation of a human figure. She closed her mind's eye to that too, though when Pug came out, he glanced quickly at her and said: "My feathered friends still need me, so I have left them what they need. And if the Baron's men should come—why, there I'll be. They'll see what they expect to see." There was challenge in his glance; yes, and amusement too. He knew that Malkin would not ask him what he meant, not because she did not know but because she *did*. It struck Malkin at that moment that perhaps she was going from the frying pan into the fire. There was much more to Pug than she had ever admitted to herself. Now, looking at the lifeless log, she thought of the spells of the People of Peace and shivered.

But Tattercoats did not notice. She had other things occupying her mind. As they began to make their way down the meadow, toward the woods, and away from the castle, Malkin saw that she was crying, silently but with some force. She moved closer to the other girl and put a tentative hand on her shoulder. Tattercoats did not shrug it away, but neither did she welcome it. She looked back once, and in her look, Malkin saw the pain of heart she was in. The castle, despite everything, had been her only home, the only place she had ever known. Of course, that was true of Malkin too, but not in the same way. The castle was Tattercoats's life, and her family. Her flight from it was an acknowledgment of betrayal, of knowledge that there was no love there for her, nothing left. There was nothing Malkin could do to help her. She knew, strongly yet inexplicably, that she must not breathe a word of what she had seen and heard at the castle the night before. Equally, she knew that Pug knew all about it, somehow.

As the day wore on, they traveled deep into the woods. They would be able to reach the other side of them by evening, and perhaps be able to camp in a barn or a hayrick in a village somewhere.

The castle of Fisher Forest would not be well known to villagers on the other side of the woods, though their lord might well know both of its existence and of the Baron, so they would be safe from pursuit as long as they kept away from any manor or castle.

In the woods it was deeply green and cool, with coins of golden light falling on the soft path. It is strange, thought Malkin. With every step my spirits rise. She had not often been in the woods, except at Maying time, when she had brought back sprays of May blossoms with the other servants, but at the moment it seemed a friendly place, full of homely, secret sounds. Pug whistled softly as he walked ahead, obviously at ease, and Tattercoats had stopped crying and walked wide-eyed, her gaze on everything. She was like a child learning to walk, thought Malkin fondly, and felt a rush of anger against the old Baron who had denied his granddaughter even this, so that she had to discover it as a grown person, not as a little child.

And then, as they came round a curve in the path, they heard something that made them stop in their tracks: a voice, singing. They were words Malkin knew, a famous song often on people's lips in those days:

> Hey ho! To the greenwood now let us go!
> Sing heave and ho! And there we will
> Find both buck and doe; sing heave and ho!
> The hart and the hind and the pretty little roe.
> Sing heave and ho! Hey ho!

Before they could stop her, Tattercoats began to sing too, joining in the round. The other voice faltered, then continued, and such was the infectious ease of it that, without knowing quite what she was doing, Malkin opened her mouth and came into the round too. As she sang, the first singer came around the curve in the path and stopped, waiting for their approach, still singing. They came together in the middle of the path, and Pug was the only one not singing. His reed was to his lips, and his whole face was changed with the music they were making. And for a while the greenwood itself was filled with a music that seemed not quite of this world, perfect in execution and melody and harmonizing voices.

At last it was ended, and there they were, foolishly stopped in the middle of a path, gawking at a stranger. The latter laughed, rubbed his eyes as if he did not quite believe what he saw, then finally took off his hat and bowed low.

"Greetings to you, birds of the wood, with your sweet noise!" he said. "Well met it is we are, indeed, like the cat said to the mouse."

"Not the words I would have chosen," said Pug, laughing too. The singer laughed again, good-humoredly. "No, indeed! I let my wish for interesting words override my good sense."

As he spoke Malkin studied him, and an arresting figure he was, indeed. Tall, very tall; broad, very broad; with hair the color of hazelnut shells, which curled haphazardly round his face; and eyes of a startling blue. He had skin well gilded by the sun, and clothes patched with so many different colors that it was hard to believe he had not constructed this odd costume on purpose. He wore one gold earring, and the top of his patched shirt was decorated with unusual swirling circular patterns. His hose were stained and of an unremarkable dun color, and his shoes had likewise seen better days. As he gestured Malkin caught sight of a ring on one of his fingers, a delicate silver ring with some flashing stone caught in its band.

"And where might you be going this fine summer day?" the stranger asked. "If you are going to the next village, do not bother. They are hardheaded, deaf-eared, flint-hearted there! I have just been there, so I know."

His tone was light but inquisitive. His voice was lovely: smooth as cream, but studded with the cloves and nutmeg of an accent Malkin could not quite place. It was a foreign one, though, of that she was quite sure.

"Where might *you* be going this fine day?" she retorted with some spirit, seeing as the other two did not seem to be making a move. "It is customary, is it not, to exchange names before the asking of impudent questions!"

The stranger looked at her and smiled. "Oh, this is the hawk speaking, who watches over her young so carefully! But sweet-voiced is this hawk and . . . I mean," he added hurriedly, seeing Malkin's expression, "I mean, Mistress, of course, how remiss of me! My name is Gallimaufry, if it pleases you, Mistress. What is Gallimaufry? Ah, well may you ask," he declared, though nobody had in fact asked, "for the fame of Gallimaufry precedes him! I am the Marquis of Motley, the Duke of Distress, the King of Poesy and Song. I am Gallimaufry," and he swept off his tattered hat again, with a lordly air, as if his words had been accompanied by a roll of the drums.

Tattercoats laughed. Gallimaufry turned to her. "And you, my pretty little wren," he said, "what is your name? Now you must tell me, since you know mine and so have power over me, and you would not be cruel, would you?"

Tattercoats, hiccuping with giggles, said, "My name is Tattercoats, and these are my friends, Malkin and Pug. We are on our way to London, Master, on our way to see the Queen."

"The Queen!" said Gallimaufry, rolling his eyes. "Oh, wren, hawk, and you, whom I must call skylark for the sweetness of your piping, you must know that the Queen does not feed the birds of the air!"

Malkin said impatiently: "It is of no concern of yours, Master, what we do. We do not ask for advice."

"Oh, but I know London, sweet hawk! It is full of traps and dangers and honey pits for little birds, and many's a one never returns to the greenwood."

All this while Pug had stood there silently, watching each in turn. Then he said, carelessly, "Why don't you come with us, then, Master Gallimaufry, and be our guide?"

Malkin turned to him, mouth open on a reproach, but Tattercoats said gaily: "Indeed, why not? The more the merrier, and already I feel much merrier than I did this morning."

So Malkin had no choice but to assent. But Gallimaufry, seeing her discomfiture, bowed low in front of her and said gravely: "Mistress Malkin, I will prove myself to be a useful companion, you will see. You will not regret having asked Gallimaufry to join your company."

Malkin shrugged, but could not help returning his smile. She noticed rather wryly, though, a short time later when they stopped under a big oak tree for their midday meal, that the young man did not seem to have any food with him. But he did not let this small embarrassment stop him from a lusty enjoyment of the cheese pies and small beer they had brought with them.

After the meal they sat and rested, while Pug played his pipe softly and Gallimaufry told them the story of his life—at least the version he wanted to tell them. He had been born long ago and far away across the western sea, he told them, and Malkin understood then that part of his accent, at least, must be Irish. She had never seen any Irish before, though she had heard stories from the head cook, who had once gone to London and seen Irish soldiers from the court of the visiting chief of Ulster, Sean O'Neill, in the street. "Such gallowglasses they were," he'd said, eyes round from the memory. "Barefooted, barelegged, clad in saffron skirts and cloaks and shirts with barbarous designs, and their hair wild and long and all over their faces, and their swords in big fringed scabbards, and wild eyes! And they were talking loudly in the street, not in a real language, but howling, like dogs!" The cook had crossed himself quickly, as if warding off an evil memory.

Now Malkin looked at Gallimaufry and listened to his winding tale and thought, why, he's nothing like them. She wondered if perhaps the cook had remembered right, or had been embroidering, as Gallimaufry was undoubtedly doing now, to Tattercoats's evident admiration. Still, she thought there might be something to the cook's words; that swaggering confidence of a lord—the silver-tongued, honey-voiced confidence of a man who was a natural prince—was strong in Gallimaufry, and though he was a boaster, he was a long, long way from being arrogant.

"By the time I was six or seven, my friends, I could already sing every tune that had ever been written, and remember the

words of any poem that had ever been written, yes, and I also
. . ."

"All that is as may be," interrupted Malkin, "but are you Irish, Gallimaufry?"

"Am I Irish?" said Gallimaufry, not missing a beat, and correctly interpreting the suddenly startled expression in Tattercoats's eyes—she had undoubtedly heard the cook's stories too. "Is the grass green? But then, ask also, Mistress Malkin, am I English? Is the sky blue?"

"It is *sometimes* blue, just as the grass is not always green," said Malkin. Then she laughed. "Oh, well, you are named Gallimaufry, so I suppose it is possible you are a medley, a mixture, a cacophony of bloods and tongues!"

"Indeed, Mistress Malkin," said Gallimaufry, his eyes thoughtful on her. Then he turned to Pug. "And you, my fine friend? You do not speak much. You watch."

"There is enough speech here for the whole of the world," said Pug, smiling. "You do not need mine as well, I think." There was an unusually satisfied expression in his eyes. He rose. "It is time to go," he said. "If we are to reach shelter for the night, we will have to walk many hours still."

"But not in that village, that cursed nest of vipers and beetles and darksome fools," said Gallimaufry, lightly getting to his own feet. "There is another village a short distance to the west of there, where I have heard people are . . . well, if not exactly sweet as violets, at least not sour like vinegar. There are some good clean barns there, and wives who will give you a drink of warm milk. I will show you the way," he added, motioning to them to follow him. "I have been a wanderer for a long time, while you greenwood birds are only just beginning."

» Eight «

They soon came to a small village just on the western flank of the wood. The cottages straggled along the edge of the narrow path, and behind them were the small fields typical of woodland villages. It was late afternoon, and the cottages were deserted. Most of the people were in the fields mowing grass, and here and there other groups of people were washing and shearing some remarkably shaggy sheep. Children ran hither and thither, the older ones helping, the younger playing shrill games.

"Wait for me here," Gallimaufry said, "for sometimes these woodlanders are the very devil for suspicion. They know me; they've seen me pass before. They know I'm no rogue."

He left them at the side of the path and walked up to the first group of shearers, who had paused in their work to watch the strangers. The others saw him advance with smiling lips and extended hands, saw the others' wariness change to recognition, although they could not hear what anyone said. Gallimaufry talked for quite a while, his hands sketching and hovering in front of him. Then he motioned to the others to come forward.

"Here are my friends," he said. "The best musicians you are ever likely to hear, short of the Royal Chapel. Tonight, my friends, we will prove it to you!" He beamed. Malkin stared. What had he said? Gallimaufry saw her look, and knitted his brows in warning.

"These good people have offered us shelter and food in return for one night's music to celebrate the end of shearing," he said. "They know we are on our way to play at the court, and that they are fortunate indeed to have our services."

"At court, is it?" said one of the shearers, a big man with a flinty look to him. "Gallimaufry, you do tell some big ones. I would like to see you appear before the Queen in all your motley!" He gave a rumbling laugh, at which his companions joined in. But there was no malice in the laughter. They evidently knew Gallimaufry well.

Gallimaufry smiled, but said: "Well may you laugh, good people, but you will see what you will see! My friend here"—pointing to Pug—"has the finest reed this side of the skylark, fairer by far than any bird you have ever heard! And my other friends—their voices will make you swoon with delight. You will not be disappointed, my friends. You will see."

Malkin caught a glimpse of Pug's face as Gallimaufry spoke. He must have felt her eyes on him, for he turned slightly to her and held her gaze for a moment. It was she who dropped her eyes first, her heart hammering a little, for in that gaze she had caught again a whisper of something she already knew—something fugitive, like a vivid dream that vanishes when you open your eyes but whose feeling lingers deep within your bones.

And so it was that much later the four of them found themselves seated at a long table under the village's apple trees, some still with late straggles of white blossom robing their branches, most with the glossy leaves of summer and the tiny fruit beginning. They were plied with good food and strong beer, jokes and good fellowship, for the prospect of a good night's dance had put all the villagers in excellent mood. But soon must come the moment of singing for supper and bed, and Malkin dreaded it. Her head was rather dizzy from the beer, her limbs heavy both from the walking they had done today and the good supper they were having. Nothing would have pleased her more than to lay her head down on a soft pillow of herbs somewhere. At her side Tattercoats chatted excitedly to this person and that, and although Malkin didn't hear all she was saying, she thought she heard her tell about the ball, and the Earl of Malmsey, and all the rest. But Malkin was too weary to tell her to hush or to be careful; in any case her audience just thought Tattercoats was spinning stories, and they listened with good humor and indulgence.

At last the big shearer who had spoken to them before rose and whispered in Gallimaufry's ear. The sun was sinking well down, and he was obviously impatient to get the entertainment going before all had to crawl off to bed. Gallimaufry got up and came around the other side of the table, where he conferred with an expressionless Pug. Then he came over to Tattercoats and, last of all, Malkin. "It is time now, I fear," he whispered. "Come, little birds, let us sing our hearts out. Let us fill these woodlanders with the joy of the open sky!"

Malkin shrugged, but Tattercoats smiled. "It will be well, Malkin, dear friend," she whispered.

"You are trusting indeed," growled Malkin, but indeed she had no choice, so she got up with the others. The villagers waited expectantly.

"Masters, mistresses, lords, ladies, never will you hear such music as you will now delight in. We four friends bring songs from the greenwood and tunes from the fields, ripples from the rivers and birdsong from the skies. We have traveled near and far, far and near, and the music of our coming still fills each hollow where our feet have trod . . ."

"He's babbling," said Malkin despairingly to Pug. Her stomach was lurching unpleasantly and her head was thick. Pug smiled and nodded, seemingly not at all disturbed. But, of course, as the only real musician among them, he had no fear of being rumbled as a cheat.

"We will proceed as at court, my four friends and I," Gallimaufry continued. "First, some poesy, then song, and music for the tripping feet." He struck an attitude, lifted his head to the sky as if trying to find inspiration there, then began:

> Bright is the brightness of my lady's hair,
> Soft is the softness of her lips so red;
> Dream of my dream is my love so fair,
> Delight on delight fills my head.

He'll not hold them long with that, thought Malkin as she watched the faces of the villagers. They wanted rough, meaty music, loud song, to forget their labor, not sickly sweet comfits of unfelt emotion. But Gallimaufry continued in the same vein, and the restlessness grew, the faces long with boredom. Malkin nudged Pug. "Pug, stop him, stop him. They will throw us out. Tell him to stop!"

But Pug did not reply. He was watching Gallimaufry carefully, his reed silent in his hand. Then he put it to his lips and began to play, the soft tendril of music curling under the words.

Gallimaufry did not pause, but the sweat that had begun to appear on his forehead beaded and dissolved down his face. He wiped it and continued, but somehow the words had changed. Something else had crept in under them, along with the questing softness of the flute's music, and this something stilled all the faces.

> But what is this? And what I hear
> Is the sound of a drum, far afield
> The sound of a drum coming so near
> The sound of a beat to which all yield;
> the sound of a pulse that will take all my mirth
> the sound of my lady's heart calling me to Earth.
> So flee, all my dreams! And flee, my delight!
> What is coming now is the soft tread of night.

And, amazingly, there *was* a pulse beating; there *was* a drum, far afield. For a frozen moment, everyone was perfectly still, as the last words died on Gallimaufry's lips, on his surprised face, and the music of the reed whispered to a dying fall with the words. But the pulse kept beating, closer now, closer, and still no one moved. Then a voice called out, a voice not rich and spicy like Gallimaufry's but rough and throaty: "Hey-ho, it is I! Is this music I hear, and I not invited! By the blue blood of le Roi Henri, it is *bonjour* to you all, and a merry night I bid you, with my drum, my *tambour, boum, boum, boum!*"

They could all see him now, coming out of the wood, a figure so twisted and dwarfish that he was even too odd for a dream. His words—spoken in the broken-glass dialect of a man not of those parts, a Frenchman no doubt, but long in England—broke the spell. There was laughter, the loud roistering laughter of relief, and the newcomer arrived in full view to the cheers and ragged joy of the villagers.

He was indeed so small and squat as to be almost a dwarf, powerfully shouldered, rather bowlegged, and dressed in unremarkable clothes. Yet when he came closer, they saw that he had a surprisingly handsome, unusually fine-boned face. His straight, bright dark hair, shot through with silver threads, was cut thickly and shortish, and he had a moustache spiky with silver and black hairs. His eyes were of a brown so dark as to be black, fringed with eyelashes so thick they could have been used to sweep bare an entire castle hall. Indeed, his head was so out of keeping with the rest of his body that it almost looked as if he were wearing one of the elaborate vizards, the masks favored by great lords at entertainments, with their gold-threaded hair and moustaches and the silk taffeta softness of their fabric cheeks.

Around his neck and hanging to his waist was a small drum, and it was this that he had been beating with such eerie effect as he came out of the woods. His powerful fists, which had been beating the drum's hide, were clenched by his side now in ironic salute as he came to a stop beside the table.

"I heard music, I knew I was called," he said. "I know if you have Pipe, you must need also Tabor." And without further ado he began to beat out a tune on the drum, in which Pug joined almost immediately on his pipe, a tune that all recognized at once as being to dance to.

Soon there was no one left at the table but Malkin, for Tattercoats and Gallimaufry had linked hands and joined the villagers dancing for sheer joy under the apple trees, with the moon rising slowly and night coming on sweetly. But even she was brought into the throng, by the big shearer who had first spoken to them, and soon forgot all else but the delight of that summer night.

» Nine «

Our travelers went on their way early the next day, their packs filled with food. They were, of course, augmented by one more member, the drummer, who called himself Tabor after his own instrument, as it was close, he said, to his own name, which no English could bring out in his mouth. He had declared that since he had nothing better to do, he had better come with them and see what good luck was to be had in London—though curse the stinking place for it was nothing like Paris and the court of le Roi Henri, as he called the French king. He had found an unexpected ally in Tattercoats, who held romantic views of the French court due to the enshrined memory of her father, Will de Montacour, whom she still believed would one day send for her.

"Tabor," she asked, "do you know my father, Will de Montacour? You must have met him! He writes me such beautiful letters."

Tabor looked at her with his beautiful eyes and said gently: "My Lady, there are many fine noblemen at le Roi Henri's court, and I am not sure that I know them all. But I am sure he is a fine man! Sure indeed!" His eyes shifted a little as he said this, and Malkin suddenly wondered just how close he had really come to the court he spoke of with such familiarity. Perhaps his stories were similar to those of Gallimaufry. But the answer seemed to satisfy Tattercoats. And really, it was the least of Malkin's worries.

It seemed to her that such a big party would only bring trouble on their heads once they reached the walls of London. The law did not like the poor to be in such rollicking numbers, and surely street musicians were deemed to be part of the rogues and vagabonds and sturdy beggars that they so disliked. But as Pug did not comment, and Gallimaufry (after his first dismay that he should be thus upstaged by another teller of tall tales) had accepted, and Tattercoats was enthusiatic, there was nothing she could do. She was beginning to feel rather superfluous, in any case. Tattercoats, fully occupied by the two who were paying what could only be called court to her, scarcely seemed to notice Malkin anymore. Malkin listened to their chatter with a wry smile.

"And then," Gallimaufry was saying, "then I went in to see that rascally innkeeper with my stick, and I began to sing one of my songs, and low and behold he started dancing. He couldn't stop, and he begged for mercy!"

"Oh," breathed Tattercoats, looking at him with wide eyes.

Tabor snorted. "And I with my drum have ended the siege of a city, merely by drumming so long and so well that terror struck into them and they flung down their arms and took to their heels!"

"Oh," said Tattercoats, smiling with immense pleasure. It was not that she encouraged these stories, but rather that she had a natural talent for making men want to pay court to her. A good talent to have, Malkin thought harshly to herself, one that will serve her well. But she could not stay cross for long. Really, the stories were so inventive, and Tattercoats's pleasure so unfeigned, that she would be a sour thing indeed if she did not respond to them.

The villagers had been quite glad to see them go, all things considered. They had had a wonderful night, but in the morning there were many sore heads around, and with the cold light of day, perhaps new constructions had been put on some of the events of the night. Indeed, the giving of their gifts of food had had rather an anxious air to it. Malkin had a distinct feeling that something would be done in the village after they left, some ritual to protect crops and children from an influence it was best not to name. Indeed, she had noticed that the man who set them on their way in the direction of the next settlement had had a small spray of rowan pinned under his cloak. Only Pug and herself seemed to notice, the others being far too busy with loud boastings to impress the untraveled Tattercoats with the relative merits of Paris, London, and Dublin.

Yes, Tattercoats was happy now. When Malkin remembered the poor girl's life back in the castle of Fisher Forest—which already seemed so far away—she thanked the stars and Pug for taking her away from it. But nevertheless it was hard to feel happy herself as she tramped along the dusty roads. She was not at all sure of what would await her on the road ahead, or if she had done a foolish thing in leaving a safe employ at a time when so many were masterless, without work, and having to live on the roads from their wits. Even if they should reach the court, and even if by some miracle or magic Tattercoats met the Earl, what then? And these two ill-matched men who walked with them now, what did they think to gain from this? And why were they here at all? They were not creatures of dream or nightmare, that was clear. They were flesh and blood, all right—Jove's bones, they were loud enough for it! Their stories piled on each other's; wanderers both, far from their native land and not quite of this one. A Frenchman born and bred and bound would have found Tabor a queer fish indeed; an Irishman of the wild Gaelic hills over the sea would have found Gallimaufry a traitor in the mind if not the flesh. Yet the label English could not quite encompass them either, so they were foreigners twice over, yet did not seem to care at all. Long years of being in this green and misty land of field and wood and village had made them understand, but not understood. A little like Pug, perhaps. *He* had always been different, always outside the common, even though he was a gooseherd. She had always thought that, for as long as she had known Pug. And how long had that been? From the first day she had been at the castle, it seemed. She creased her forehead in thought. That was at least seven years ago, for she had come to the castle when she was nearly ten.

They stopped by a pretty little river, and the two girls left the men and walked upstream a little to where hanging willows made a place of privacy. They undressed and went rather gingerly into the water, gasping at its cool shock on their sweaty bodies. But after a short while, they were swimming out to the other side, where a deep waterhole gave pleasurable diving and splashing. They swam back to their clothes slowly, lazily, in no hurry to get back downstream. As they emerged, water rolling off shoulders, backs, thighs, and hair, Tattercoats said, laughing, "All we need now, Malkin, is some sweet perfume and creams to anoint ourselves with!"

Malkin grinned. "Is that all? Sweet perfume, creams, oils—conjured from the air?"

"Maybe if we wish," Tattercoats said, "if we really wish." Her eyes shone. "Things come to us, Malkin. They do. I know that now."

Malkin was about to make some witty retort when she caught sight of a woman sitting on the bank watching them, her arms around her drawn-up knees. This woman could have seemed elderly, with hair as white as snow and black taffeta skirts, but her cheeks were like fat apples, rosy and unwrinkled, and her eyes shone with youthful sparkle.

"Creams, oils, and unguents, is it, my little ladies?" she called as they bolted for their clothes. From under the flurried fall of her shift, Malkin saw that the woman had risen and was coming toward them carrying a small wooden case, such as an apothecary or healer might have.

Tattercoats was at her side in a moment. "Oh, what do you have in your case? Oh, show us, do!"

It came to Malkin that Tattercoats was being schooled in sweet expectancy, in always trusting to the bounty and protection of others. But then, had that not always been one of the most lovable things about her?

The woman's star-bright eyes twinkled at Tattercoats. "Yes, my little lady, you look and see what I have for you! Dame Pennyroyal is my name, and royal treatment is what you will get from me, Mistresses . . ."

"Tattercoats and Malkin," Tattercoats said, her words tumbling eagerly over each other. She was already peering into the open case. "Oh, look!"

The case was divided into several compartments, each lined with violet cloth. Inside was a plethora of little bottles and jars, including some so tiny you could have comfortably held them in the crook of your little finger. The glass bottles held liquids, each of a different color—from saffron yellow to madder scarlet, from gentian violet to a green as deep as spring grass. The jars were made of fired pottery, each carefully labeled in tiny brown handwriting.

"Here is sweet sorrel salve," Dame Pennyroyal said, pulling out a little jar. "One dab of this behind your ear and you'll hear the sweetest music that was ever made. Here . . ." lifting out a bottle of scarlet liquid, "is love-in-idleness-no-more, which will cause a man to fall in love with you instantly. And here . . ." pulling out a tiny bottle of deep golden liquid, "is ambergold, the rarest perfume in all the world! It comes from the deepest caves in the world, by the shores of the deepest sea. It has all the fires of the earth and the beauty of the stars, and she who wears it becomes instantly a magnet for all eyes. She could be in rags and tatters and still no one would notice. Well, what is it to be, my Lady?"

"Oh . . ." breathed Tattercoats. "Oh, do I have to decide?"

"We cannot pay you," Malkin said briskly, finding her voice at last, "so it is useless to try and sell to us."

Tattercoats looked as if she'd been slapped.

Dame Pennyroyal looked reproachfully at Malkin. "Who spoke of payment, Mistress?" she said. "I sell to whom I want, and I give to whom I want." She looked firmly at Tattercoats. "You do not have to decide," she said. "You can have a bit of each."

At that moment came the sweet notes of Pug's pipe. Malkin said, laughing, "There is no need for the sweet sorrel salve, Dame Pennyroyal."

"Indeed, indeed," said Dame Pennyroyal, not in the least flustered and dabbing a fingertip of salve behind Tattercoats's ear. "With this you will hear even sweeter." Without a glance at the approaching men, she picked up the second bottle, that of love-in-idleness-no-more.

Malkin observed, without thinking, "You should not use that till we see the Earl of Malmsey."

The woman's bright eyes snapped and sparked even more at Malkin's words, but she did not ask any questions. Instead, she carefully stoppered the bottle again. "You are right; we will wait," she said. She picked up the third bottle just as the men reached them. "But this one, ambergold perfume, she must wear. It will make all who see her forget about her rags and tatters . . ."

"Oh, but oh . . ." said Tattercoats, and blushed. "Oh, but I could still see I'm in rags and tatters, Dame Pennyroyal."

"That is a problem," agreed the herbalist. "It may be possible for me to mix up something that will do both. But it will take time."

"And time is what we do not have overmuch of," said Malkin.

"Mistress Tattercoats needs no perfume to disguise her," said Gallimaufry. "Her rags and tatters are as lace and cobweb and dew on the fairest flower of all . . ."

"I have seen ladies of the court of le Roi Henri dressed in rags, yes, besides Mistress Tattercoats," said Tabor.

The two men looked at each other and at Tattercoats, well pleased with their game of cap-the-compliment. But it was Pug who said, "Come with us, Dame Pennyroyal, and we will see what we will see."

Malkin opened her mouth to argue, then closed it. One more, one less, it made no difference. As they made ready to go once more, the herbalist softly called Malkin over. "My unguents and salves, Mistress—they may not be magic, but they do no harm. If a young girl smells as good as a garden of roses, there is no harm in that, is there, only joy? And Mistress Malkin, you may find I am useful in more ways than one later."

Malkin glanced sharply at Dame Pennyroyal. "It is not my doing whether you come or stay," she said. "One or three, what does it matter?"

≫ ≫   ≪ ≪

And so it was that they set off again on their journey to the great city of London. As they walked they talked: of Fisher Forest and the Baron and Oscuro and the ball of the Earl of Malmsey. But also they sang many songs, the chorus of their voices ringing along the road, punctuated by Tabor's drum and Pug's pipe.

Part Two

Midsummer Court

» Ten «

They were weary. The road stretched endlessly in front of them, miles of silver gray dust and stones. It was not easy walking, for every few minutes they had to leave the reasonably well-made middle of the road and retreat to its ragged edges as carriages, carts, and horsemen sped past them, dust flying out from under hooves and wheels, choking the travelers. It seemed the world was going to London that day! Overhead the sky was of that crystal blueness, thickening to a pearly haze near the horizon, that usually meant you would have been drenched by a summer storm late afternoon. They had started out early, but the day had become steadily hotter, and the glare, the dust, and the sharp little stones finding their way into their thinning shoes had become steadily more unbearable. Even Gallimaufry, Tabor, and Pennyroyal, who were not nervous of the heavy traffic like Malkin and Tattercoats, were starting to look rather wilted. Only Pug walked on with exactly the same step as he'd started out with, the light, limping step that should have tired him quicker than the others but somehow did not.

At last Tattercoats said: "I'm stopping. I cannot bear walking anymore." She walked off the road, down the edge, out of the ditch, and onto the field beyond, where she flopped down and closed her eyes. The others followed. For a moment no one spoke; they were too busy catching their breath. Malkin closed her eyes. Little golden dust motes danced in front of her closed lids, and shafts of black lightning. Her head felt light and full of a strange spinning, and her belly was uncomfortably empty. There would be nothing to eat till they came to the next village.

Silence. Only the rush and whoosh of wheels on the road told them the world was going on without them. And what a rushed, busy world! Very few of the travelers on that road had paused for even so much as a good day; they all seemed too intent on their business. For Malkin, brought up in Fisher Forest where hardly any visitors came, it was almost incredible that strangers should not be interested in others. Perhaps, she thought with a thumping of her heart, there were so *many* strangers in London that there was no one else: no friends, no families. Oh, but that was silly! Slowly, as the vague confusion of thoughts filled her head, she began to relax, to allow the weariness to flow from her limbs.

And then Gallimaufry began to sing, softly:

Our footsteps ring upon the road;
Oh, who will light this heavy load?
For fleet of foot we are, and strong;
But oh, the road it is so long!

That is what poets do, she thought vaguely. They turn everything into song. At first his voice was uncertain, fumbling to find the tune to fit the words into like a glove to a hand, but then Pug's pipe took up the melody surely, and softly Tabor's drum began to beat. Gallimaufry sang the words again, the melody grew and grew under Pug's gentle fingers and Tabor's fists, and soon they were all sitting up singing this new song, mightily pleased with themselves and one another. Over and over they sang it, tripping in and out of high and low voices, just for the sheer pleasure of it. And when it was finished, they were as refreshed as if they had had a plunge into a clear river. Tattercoats spoke for them all when she said, clasping her hands together: "Oh, my friends! How I wish it could always be like this!"

Now the walking had a rhythm to it, a song, and as she walked, Malkin said the words to herself, while Pug's pipe kept playing the melody. Even when three carriages swept past them in quick succession and the air turned to roiling, choking dust, blotting out the road before and behind the rumbling wheels, she was still happy, the words singing in her mind. But it was really too much when, after they had just set foot on the road again, along came another blinding, glittering dust storm carried under wheels. This time the carriage had come up so fast they barely had time to fling themselves on the wayside. Half-blinded, coughing, and spluttering, Malkin scrambled to her feet at last— to find that the dust had thinned because the carriage had stopped. She opened one eye and blinked. She shook her head as if to clear it, and opened both eyes wide to see a large carriage drawn by four beautiful bay horses, and a large driver in the act of jumping down from his vehicle. He came running to them, his ruff splendidly yellow-starched, his doublet and hose of some magnificent silver-threaded green stuff. "Forgive me, forgive me," he panted, his face as red as a ripe strawberry, "I came as quickly as I *could* come." He bowed low. "At your service."

Malkin looked quickly at the others and received a severe shock, for they were all gone, and in their place stood four strangers, four splendidly dressed strangers: a young woman in a white and silver dress, her hair high-swept above a spangled gauze ruff, a string of mist-white and rain-lucid stones around her neck, set on the fine grain of her well-displayed white bosom; a much older woman in a magnificent russet taffeta dress, waisted with a fine velvet girdle set with carefully worked gold links and from which hung several small jewels and even a small silver watch; a young man dressed in the height of fashion—but not ridiculously, like Oscuro had been—his legs well turned in their pale silk hose, his waist shown to full advantage, his hair curling and glittering with many lights; and a slightly older man in deep red velvet and silk, with a French hat, a rapier hanging from his side, and even a pistol in his belt. Malkin took a step backward, then saw that these were her friends—amazingly changed, but still her friends. There was Tattercoats's sweet smile above the gauzy ruff; and there were Dame Pennyroyal's quick fingers, feeling at her unaccustomed finery; and there was Gallimaufry, his handsomeness now undeniable; and Tabor, his drum still dangling from his neck, rather incongruously over his gallant's finery. She saw the shock in their eyes and, looking down at herself, saw that she was changed too. She had on a dress of deep, almost midnight blue, silk and velvet, inset with panels of paler blue satin. Around her neck hung a heart-shaped gold pendant on a thin golden chain. She felt her hair: it had been swept up, like Tattercoats's, and at the top of it, she could feel a cap of velvet set with little round stones that must be pearls. She dropped her hand.

They all looked at one another. Nobody could speak. Then suddenly Tattercoats laughed. "We are like mooncalves, staring at each other!" she said. "And we are making our driver wait too long with our foolish stares! Come, the coach is waiting and we must go!"

But Pug, where was Pug? Malkin turned. And there he was, his clothes of the same silver-threaded green as the driver's, but somehow on him they seemed like a disguise, like they didn't fit. She thought she could still see the old Pug under there, unchanged. He saw her look and said, laughing: "Come, Malkin. You heard our friend. And look, they are gone already."

And indeed the others, quite forgetting their new dignity, were running toward the carriage, their steps almost those of a dance, so happy did they seem.

"But . . . but . . ." Malkin wanted to ask a thousand questions. Her heart raced as if it had already joined the others in their flight toward the new life.

Pug put a finger to his lips. "It is not time," she thought she heard him murmur as he beckoned her urgently toward the waiting carriage.

» Eleven «

The carriage smelled of scented wood and new cloth, and for quite a while, the joy of their new surroundings filled their hearts. In velvet pouches in their clothes, each found gold coins such as they had never thought to see, much less to handle; the coins engraved with Saint Michael and the dragon, known as angels; the sovereigns, with their picture of the Queen; and the big royals, with their image of majesty. The coins clinked against each other with a cheery metallic sound, and they laughed to hear them. Under their feet they found cunningly worked baskets full of fragrant little dishes, and they lost no time in enjoying the roast meats, nut tarts, plump fruit, and sweet comfits that they contained. It was like a dream, but if dream it were, they did not want to wake up. A dream dreamed by so many was a dream that could be made to last, but a dream questioned was one that could shatter into crystal pieces of enchantment, each irretrievably lost to the others.

They talked not of what had been but of what was to be, for within their cocoon of silk and wood, they could see the road still stretching, but they were now lords of it. When the rain came, as it had looked like it would, it drummed obediently on the roof of the carriage without making so much as a splash on their joy, and indeed they laughed to see it fall. At last, tired, excited, and, deep down, rather nervous of what had happened to them, they fell asleep.

Only Pug stayed awake, and he sat quietly in a corner of the carriage, his pipe to his lips, very, very softly playing. The thin thread of sweet sound wound through Malkin's dreams as she reclined on the soft cushions. Once she opened one eye and almost cried out, for she thought the dream had quite ended, but

Pug played on, and slowly the eye closed and she went properly to sleep. Outside, the steady clattering of the horses' hooves on the road and the first confused murmurings of the big city told of the real world still to be faced, but inside the carriage sweet, golden sleep hung heavily, like a brocade curtain drawn over the first act of a play.

» » « «

They woke as the carriage rattled its way in between the city gates. Now they sat up and looked out of the windows. Such noise, such bustle! Tattercoats snapped a wide-eyed look at Malkin, for neither of them had ever imagined anything so big, so crowded. Cries floated in to them on the golden afternoon air:

"Hot peas!"

"Hot fine oatcake!"

"Ho, now, what do you lack, what do you lack, gentlemen and ladies?"

"Small coals, small coals!"

"Buy a mat, a mat, a fine mat!"

"Whiting, maids, whiting!"

"Have you any old boots? Ho, now, any old boots?"

"New brooms, green brooms, fine brooms and handy!"

Add the hubbub of voices, the tramp of feet, the rumble of wheels, church bells ringing, beggars with their bowls clacking, children bawling, dogs howling—was it any wonder that the girls felt almost deafened?

"I could make a song of this, by Jove's bones, yes I could!" said Gallimaufry excitedly. "This is the life for me, friends! You can keep your field and forest!"

For a moment a sharp nostalgia for the quiet meadows and green woods of her home seized Malkin, then it left her in the excitement of the new. And the others, she saw, had none of that brief nostalgia; they were all for the pleasure of the moment, for the brilliant spell, or dream, or what you will, that had fallen on them and that they did not want to break. But the questions Malkin had left far behind on the dusty road now began to catch up with her other thoughts. She looked across at

Pug, who alone was not craning his neck to see. He smiled and raised his eyebrows, and she knew she would have no answers from him today.

"We shall have to go to the Thames," Gallimaufry said. "In this city, the streets are well-nigh choked. The river is the only way to go if we are to get anywhere near the palace."

Tabor crossed his arms. "In Paris one must go by the Seine," he agreed, "for it is similar there. Yet I have heard that this Thames of yours is as murky as a pond and that your watermen are cheats and liars, so we must beware."

"Oh ho," retorted Dame Pennyroyal, *"Monsieur,* you can stop your fine airs, for the Thames runs in my blood, it does indeed, and I do know that her watermen are strong and free, not like your milk-blooded French boatmen on that trickle of sour water you call a river back over the Channel!" Her color was high; her eyes sparkled.

Tabor said, angrily, "They are in fine fettle, good lady, but then so am I . . ."

"Please, my friends, let us not quarrel over such trifles," Tattercoats said hastily. "I am sure both the Thames and the Seine are fine rivers indeed; oh, and I have not seen either!" She clasped her hands. "But I will see one today! Is that not the finest thing in all the world?"

"There is much to see," Gallimaufry said, as the others subsided, their ruffled feathers forgotten. "The *Golden Hind,* that sails no more under Drake but now keeps a sharp supper table. We could float past the Tower and see London Bridge, though we must go on land near there for fear of her arches. Over the river from Saint Paul's are the Bear Gardens, and the Globe, where I do hear the world passes. And then in Saint Paul's Churchyard is my favorite place—oh, the booksellers and printers! So many books you would not think the world had so many! And then down the Thames we could float again, and . . ."

"Stop! Stop!" Tattercoats had her hands over her ears, laughing. "Dear Sir Gallimaufry, you do fill my head with all these words! I do not know any of the places, and all will be new to me and marvelous. We shall ask the driver if he can tell us a good place to eat. London sounds like a place to give a body a good stomach for the best food."

She even talks differently, Malkin thought, amazed. Her voice was surer; her eyes danced. She was still the same dear, dear Tattercoats with her sweet looks, but what a difference the fine clothes had made to her confidence! There was no need to worry about how she would be at court; her manner said she would be a success, or at least know what to do. Tattercoats was a born lady, of course, and now that could be seen properly. She was like a jewel whose true brilliance is not seen when it comes dull from the earth, even though its worth is sure, but, set in gilt and polished, it shines with a thousand fires. A diamond: that was she.

"A jeweled future for our girl, then, Malkin?" The whisper came from beside her, from Pug, who was watching with a small smile.

Malkin started. She said, "I think so, do you not, Pug?" She paused, and their eyes met. Slowly she said, "But you *know*, don't you, Pug? You *know* what's going to happen."

He raised his eyebrows. "I know no more than you, Malkin. Or little more."

"Are we in a dream, Pug?" she asked suddenly. "Or a spell? Will it end? Will we find ourselves dusty on the road, in our tatters?"

"Why ask me? You can see as well as I," he said, and grinned at her annoyance.

» Twelve «

The river was even more crowded than they had imagined. Graceful light ships, clumsy barges, and fast little wherries—rowing boats carrying passengers and goods—plied up and down its majestic waters. The air was filled with the strong smells of a busy waterway, the shouts of dockers loading and unloading, and boatmen calling out for passengers: "Eastward Ho!" and "Westward Ho!" Taverns of all kinds were huddled by the docks and the public stairs, and in all of her life, Malkin had never imagined the extraordinary variety of humanity that passed raucously by. There were swaggering gallants and rascally sailors; men with a desperate air, others with lordly grimaces; women with brawny arms and even brawnier voices; dark-skinned, turbaned grandees; and slash-cheeked London nips and foists, as cutpurses and pickpockets were known.

"Come, come." Pug's voice seemed to come from a great distance, carried on a thread of music. Malkin, looking wildly around, discovered she was alone. She stepped briskly out of the carriage, and as her feet touched the ground, saw that she was back to her old clothes. She looked back to the carriage—just in time to see it vanishing as quickly as if it had been plucked out of the air. A shiver hit her like a quake. But she had no time to ponder, for there was Pug, grinning impatiently, his reed just lowered from his lips. "Malkin, my Malkin," he said, "you will be missed if you do not hurry." And indeed Malkin could just glimpse the backs of the others, clad once again in their old clothes. Pug made her rush until they came directly to the public stairs leading to the place where a great number of wherries of different sizes were tied up, waiting for hire. As they caught up to the others, Pug forestalled her questions by saying, "No one will remember us in rags. It is all a matter of seeing, Malkin." His eyes flicked just behind them, back into the warren of streets. Malkin glanced back there quickly, and at first saw nothing, then something that made her heart beat faster. Was that? No . . . yes, yes, it was a coach, struggling through the blocked street, heavy, dark, painted with a coat of arms she recognized. A spear, a trident, a tree—it was the arms of the Baron of Fisher Forest! And if that were so, then . . .

"But *he* knows us like this," she cried urgently. "He would not know us in our finery!"

Pug smiled. "Look at the crowds," he observed. "Would you see a few sparrows among so many? But a peacock catches the eye."

There were peacocks aplenty in the crowd, Malkin wanted to say. But there was no time, for the others, apparently not disturbed by their sudden retransformation, were beckoning. They had decided on four small westwardbound wherries, and the boatmen were looking impatient about going. They made their money on the quick ferrying of passengers to and fro, and so did not like to waste time in between transactions.

Gallimaufry yabbered knowledgeably with one of them, a tough, gaunt beanpole who appeared to have some influence with the other three. "Now take us as far as London Bridge," he said earnestly, "then leave us at the Billingsgate wharf."

"You don't want to shoot the bridge?" said the boatman, with a straight face. "It is quite a . . ."

"No, no," said Gallimaufry, smiling. "I have been here before! You can pick us up again at the public stairs some time after. We want to see the town!"

"Aye, you want to see the town," said the boatman. "First show us the color of your money. Four pennies, even though you are five, to be divided between each of us. The best value in London, for you pay not by number of passengers but by wherry! But you must pay now."

"Four pennies!" said Tabor grandly, before Malkin could correct the man on his passenger arithmetic. "Pah!" He rummaged in the pouch that hung from his dilapidated belt and pulled out a handful of . . . leaves. He handed a fistful to the boatman, who did not punch him as Malkin had expected. Indeed, he grinned—a wide, wide grin that showed his few remaining teeth. "Why, moonsieur!" he said in a dreadful attempt at a French accent, sketching a bow to Tabor. "Moonsieur is really too kind, *oui!*" He then did an amazing thing: he gave a couple of leaves to his fellow boatmen and pocketed the others, with every appearance of great satisfaction. Malkin stared, then looked sharply at Pug, who shrugged. She heard his whisper: "The glamour is upon them, Malkin. Only you can truly see. But wait a moment, for all wears off. In time all glamour vanishes. . . ."

"Well, my fine sirs and ladies, get in, get in, and we will get you to the bridge in a trice!"

Well, Malkin thought, if Thames boatmen are satisfied with leaves as payment, London must truly be in another world! Marveling, she got into the biggest wherry, the one belonging to the boatman who had done most of the talking, with Tattercoats and Pug, while the other three went one each to the smaller wherries. And then they were off, skimming over the water as the boatman displayed tremendous skill and reckless speed, dodging other traffic, weaving in and out of the waterlanes with every appearance of nonchalance. Not so Malkin and Tattercoats, who clung wide-eyed to the sides of the boat, occasionally closing their eyes in terror as they whizzed past the bow of a much bigger craft.

Nobody spoke; the boatman concentrated on the water, his passengers on hanging on. Once, the boatman called out, "Look, there, the Tower!" And there it was, grimly rising from its gardens that came down to the water's edge. Here it was that important prisoners were kept before their dawn executions, treaties were signed, the crown jewels were held, coins were minted, weapons were stocked, and marriages were performed! Over the water came a cacophony of strange sounds: not human sounds but the wild, fearful howling and roaring of exotic animals, terror-stricken at finding themselves captive; lions, bears, and more, savage prisoners of the Tower too.

Malkin and Tattercoats could not keep from staring, but Pug did not even look. He had his reed to his lips and played softly. The tune he played seemed out of kilter with this roaring, lusty place, its sound as sweet and lost as the skylark hurtling up from the grass. Malkin's eyes suddenly smarted. She looked across at dreamy Tattercoats and all at once she knew, with a sudden sharp clarity that tore into her, that she was indeed the only one, apart from Pug, who saw things as they truly were, the only one to see past the glamour and ask questions. But she did not know why. It made her feel alone, especially when Pug did not give any straight answers, just riddles. The clarity lasted for a few moments, then, blink, it was gone.

And as the clarity vanished, they passed by Customs House and floated past the docks of Billingsgate, where baskets of slippery silver fish, high-piled grain, salted meat, and jeweled tumbles of fruit were being landed and sorted. And thence to London Bridge, so vast and towering that they gave an involuntary gasp. The boatman, slowing down, gave a proud grin. "You'll not have seen anything like this before," he said firmly, and they nodded, looking at the great breadth of the piers, the vast grain mills that blocked some of the openings, the narrow arches, the crowds of people and carts passing continually. The boatman drew into the public stairs and, leaning on his oars, said, "For another silver coin, ladies, I can shoot those arches for you and land you in Southwark without getting your feet wet!" Their looks of panic, their scrambling to their feet and hasty retreat amused him greatly, for he stood there holding his sides and laughing for quite some time.

» Thirteen «

Is it a lord I am? Or just a dream?
Do I sleep? If that I seem
Not to know, and ask of you
To tell the truth, and tell it true,
Why then, I speak, I know, I see;
I hear a pleasant melody . . .
Away, away shake off my sleep,
and hold to what I keep:
My foolish fancies are no more,
For I live now, who did but dream before . . .

Gallimaufry sang his song as they walked through the streets
away from the river, heading toward Saint Paul's Churchyard.
Malkin saw that he was looking at Tattercoats as he sang. And
that she looked dreamily back at him.

"Perhaps this would be a pretty song to sing before the
Earl of Malmsey," said Malkin sharply, making both Tattercoats and
Gallimaufry start. Tattercoats fiddled nervously at the place
where her necklace should have been . . . *was?* For now there
it was again, mist-white and rain-lucid stones on the gleaming
ivory of her breast. Malkin blinked, shook her head, looked down
at herself. She felt the deep silk, her own hand rustling it, and
looked up to see Pug's smile, and to hear the melody that coun-
terpointed Gallimaufry's song.

And look, yes, there it was: their coach, there on the street
as if it had always been there, and they climbed in, laughing, and
around them passersby surged and stared, then passed on their
way as Londoners will. No, none of them argued or questioned.
For you did not argue with a dream or a spell: you lived it. And

with a queer sense of rightness, they knew that the coach would sweep them, all six of them, along the busy streets in a rushing quietness on the cobblestones. Gallimaufry sang his song again, and this time there was no mistaking the love in his eyes and Tattercoats's answering passion, nor Tabor's and Pennyroyal's melancholy glances of indulgence, as if each remembered something far back in their past.

Suddenly, from her vantage point in the high vehicle, Malkin could see the river again; she could see, as if in a play, a small scene down there on the wharf below: their boatman, gaunt, tough, gesticulating, his hands opening and shutting convulsively, and inside them . . . leaves, leaves! She smiled despite herself, and looked at Pug to see if he was enjoying the joke, but he was quiet and serious. His eyes said, "Look again," and so she did.

Down with the boatman, there was someone else, golden-splendid and ridiculous—deadly as a wasp, a droning knight on his way to the Queen. Oscuro! Oscuro with the honey tongue and the poison eyes that were looking up, away from the river, into the town. She shrank back, even though he would not see them in the coach. How could he? But the sight of him was enough to dissolve the cocoon of safety in which they were protected by Pug's . . . magic? Yes, for that is what it must have been. He had said they were protected by the Other Country, but they were there now, no? A country not of field and forest but of crowd and cutpurse, of court and cozeners, of high tower and high dudgeon, of wild animals not of the silent woods but of the dense forests of the human heart.

She saw, before they turned the corner, Oscuro striding away from the wharf, the boatman yelling, and a coin flung back at him. Just as they passed out of sight, she saw the man pick it up and examine it carefully. Oh yes, she thought, more than likely he'll be biting it and getting a sore tooth for his pains, for he would never trust coin or his own sly bargains again. It would have made Malkin laugh a few seconds ago—and if there had been no jeweled insect responsible for it. As it was, she thought, they had made an enemy of the boatman, which was not wise.

She turned to Pug, but he was chatting brightly with Dame Pennyroyal and Tabor—or at least brightly agreeing with their chatter.

"And I have found, my lad, that cowslip and violet and purslane and primrose make a good salad, and pretty as a picture fresh painted. And good for the heart, the liver, and the melancholy sadness. Have you tried it now, my lad?"

"Oh yes," said Pug. "I have indeed."

"In my country," said Tabor proudly, "at the court of le Roi Henri, there are such salads as are so beautiful that they must needs hold them under glass and preserve them for all *prosperity*. Truly they are, Mistress. It would gladden your heart to see them! And you too, my boy!"

"I'm sure it would," said Pug, and he winked at Malkin.

Tattercoats and Gallimaufry added nothing to this conversation, just kept looking at each other. But what of the Earl? The Earl of Malmsey for whose sake and pretty waist—not to speak of pretty chest, aye, pretty chest full of gold—they had come so far? Tomorrow was his birthday and the day of the ball. So Tattercoats must not look at any ragged Erse, even if he were not ragged right now, for she would be a countess, not the mistress of the Marquis of Motley, the Duke of Distress, the King of Rags and Tatters.

And then Tattercoats sighed and turned her eyes away. She did not speak of what ailed her, but Malkin thought she knew. She was probably thinking of her grandfather, and how pleased he would be if she married the Earl, that he might even come to love her. . . . She was a girl who never revised her good opinions if she could help it, it was just too much trouble to think at all. Oh, horror, said Malkin to herself. Just because you think unkindly, that does not mean Tattercoats does so! So what if poor Tattercoats thinks gently of the wicked Baron. That might be enough to redeem him in the end. It might even be enough to forgive him Oscuro. But then, the Italian magician had done very little, still. Perhaps he was all buzz and no sting, all drone and no honeycomb.

At last the coach stopped near the walls of Saint Paul's Churchyard, and Gallimaufry eagerly jumped off and held out his arm, gallantlike, to Tattercoats, who came out in a sweet confusion.

If the streets had seemed full, it was as nothing to the boiling mass that swirled in here. On every side were great houses, each with bookshops attached, and stalls overflowing with more books than Malkin had ever thought existed in the whole world.

"New books, new books! What do you lack, gentlemen? A new book!" was called out from everywhere, and when they elbowed their way through the eager buyers and even more eager sellers and came to the great cathedral, well, there they saw such sights as would have caused some to throw up their hands in horror. In the central aisle, called Duke Humphrey's or Paul's walk, men gesticulated: lawyers at their pillars arguing their cases, and masterless workers touting for service. And in the rood loft, furtive messengers received and gave money, and assignations were made! Once, not long ago, even food and horses had been sold here, with a great clattering of hooves and the stink of horse flesh and the cries of fowls filling a place that was meant to be holy. At length the Lord Mayor grew angry and banned the livestock. But still Saint Paul's was the place where you could come if you needed a special service done—for all manner of uneasy types lurked here. Some of them were there now—men with bold, dangerous stares—and Malkin quickly pushed her way out again, followed by the others.

It was good to be out of the stifling, sweaty dark and into the day again. Out in the dusty liveliness of the booksellers' churchyard, Malkin hurried to a stall just to escape the memory of those arrogant stares. She hardly saw the pimpled little clerk selling his tumbling wares. She picked up a book. *Holinshed Chronicles* she would have read on the cover if she had been able to read. A handsome cover it had indeed, all brown-tooled leather, and so it should, for it cost a shilling. The pimpled boy said: "Your lord will love this book, my Lady. You must buy it." Malkin searched quickly in her plump pouch for the necessary silver coin. Not leaf now, so she handed it over and left, but not before bumping into a shortish, dark-haired man with sharp hazel eyes. He was obviously a known customer, but not perhaps a rich or important one, for the pimpled clerk said, in a tone nicely familiar: "Good day to you, Master Shakespeare! What would you like today?"

Malkin hurried on, book under arm. It was the first she had ever possessed, and she felt its strange bulkiness keenly. She did not know what she would do with it, for what was a book if it was not read? She opened it and flapped one of the pages, almost laughing at the sight of the busy words scurrying like ants all over it. What was their purpose? Shut inside the book, they were trapped; when you opened it up, there they were, urgent feelers waving. Maybe she would ask someone to teach her to read, and so she could put the ants out of their misery.

She found the others at the corner of the churchyard, ready and waiting for her. Gallimaufry had a hillock—no a *mountain*—of musty, dusty books.

"New songbooks!" he said gaily. "And Spenser's description of Ireland. Though it be mostly lies, it reminds me of the old country."

"I have a new treatise on swords," said Tabor importantly.

"And I the newest herbal," said Pennyroyal, flourishing a heavy tome. They exclaimed over Malkin's *Holinshed,* even Tattercoats, who had not bought one book but stood gazing proudly at Gallimaufry and his dusty bundle.

As they climbed into the coach, Malkin saw out of the corner of her eye the dark-haired man she had seen before, staring in their direction. She felt a sudden rush of fear: was he one of Oscuro's creatures? But gradually she realized he was staring at Pug, and that a smile was touching the corner of his lips, a smile of dawning—but surely mistaken—recognition. He had no time to call out or do anything at all, for the coach, in a second, had swished out of sight, heading for Fleet Street and the Strand. Malkin worried on the tiny moment for a short while, but soon other thoughts overtook her. Tomorrow evening was the Earl's birthday ball: an auspicious night indeed, for it would be midsummer.

» Fourteen «

Nobody had seemed at all surprised when the coach drew up at a beautiful black-and-white turreted house. The coachman had opened the door with a flourish, and bowed. "Home, my lords and ladies," he had said.

Gallimaufry had taken Tattercoats's arm. "My Lady Susanna," he had said softly, "will you do me the honor?" And the others had followed in their stately wake, Malkin and Pug last of all. There had been a queer feeling in Malkin's throat, a kind of thickness made up of excitement and melancholy in almost equal parts. She had heard Pug say gently, "This is what we wanted, isn't it, Malkin?" and she had nodded, unable to speak, unable to confess to her own confusion. Oh, if only she could be as innocent and accepting of enchantment as the others! They just enjoyed it; she questioned its every manifestation.

Now she watched Tattercoats as the other girl stood despondently in her linen shift at the window, her hair like a lick of flame down her pearly back. On the bed behind her lay a splendid dress of silver and grape-skin silk, so splendid indeed that it seemed almost a creature in its own right, reposing there on the bedcover in stiff majesty. Under the dress was a pair of silver shoes, so finely chased and fashioned that they looked as if they were spun out of the finest Venetian glass. Near the dress was laid out a carcanet of silver chains, and rubies as red as the deepest fires of the earth.

These were not the clothes of even a knight's daughter, but those of a veritable princess, a princess of some unknown, extraordinary foreign land. Yet Malkin thought they were not a patch on the feather dress and the shoes of rushes.

"You must be ready very soon," Malkin said. "The coach is coming in a short time."

Tattercoats did not answer. She had dismissed with an impatient hand the maids who had attempted to dress her, gesturing that she wanted just Malkin with her. It seemed the habit of command was an easy one for her to acquire.

"What is wrong?" Malkin asked patiently, suppressing a deep sigh. The servants had acted as if they had orders that only Tattercoats and Gallimaufry, Pennyroyal and Tabor were going to the ball. They had not offered Malkin or Pug any help, and there were no magnificent new clothes waiting for them. Malkin tried not to care. But it was still bitter to know that you were forever helper and never helped, especially when three Johnny-come-latelies could thrust their hands into the cornucopia of blessings bestowed on Tattercoats.

Tattercoats did not reply for a moment, then she turned suddenly back to face Malkin, her hair swinging around her. "I do not need the Earl of Malmsey," she exclaimed, her eyes filling with tears. "I do not know him; I do not want to know him! I want to go back to Fisher Forest with . . . with one who is more worthy. My grandfather will see that kind hearts are better than coronets!"

Malkin smiled despite herself. "No, *my Lady Susanna*," she said meaningfully. "You must follow this to the end and go to the ball. Who knows, though? You might indeed prove that kind hearts are better than coronets, and marry your true love."

As well to expect hens to start reciting poetry or pigs to dance the galliard, she thought, as to think that the Baron of Fisher Forest would be moved by a naive girl. He was not wise enough for that; it was much easier for such a one to be gulled by rapacious cozeners who thought only of lining their own pockets.

"Do you think so, Malkin?" Tattercoats—Susanna—searched her friend's face. "I know you would not lie to me." She walked rapidly forward and clasped Malkin's hand. "You would not, would you, Malkin?"

Tears pricked most treacherously under Malkin's own eyelids as she looked at the other girl's open, hopeful face. "Of course I would not, my Lady Susanna," she said, fiercely.

"Please," Tattercoats said, shivering, "don't call me that. It makes me feel strange, as if I had vanished, had been cast by a spell into something I am not."

Malkin looked at her. "But we *are* under a . . ." she began, when Tattercoats interrupted her.

"Please," she said, and Malkin saw that tears were brightening her eyes. "This is all like a beautiful dream, but . . . oh, Malkin, it makes me afraid! I don't want to wake up from it, back into my ordinary life. But I am afraid, too, that if I don't wake up, that means I have been spirited into another world from where I can never return. It's better then not to ask questions, not to know . . . I'm not sure of what I'm saying, Malkin, but do you understand? Say you do, dear Malkin. Say you do. You always seem to know, to see further than me. Malkin . . ." And she touched her friend's arm impulsively, the tears still shining in her eyes.

And then Malkin understood that the other girl had indeed been affected by all the magic changes that had gone on, but had thought that if she spoke of it, it would wear off, like a dream vanishes from the sleeper when she wakes. To accept and not question: that was the rule in dreams. And perhaps, if one followed the rule, the dream would not vanish but might become waking reality. And that meant not disturbing the dreammaker by trying to possess the dream, by forcing it to follow your terms and not its own. That was why Tattercoats did not want to be called my Lady Susanna when it was for Tattercoats that good fortune had come playing his pleasant melody.

Malkin smiled, her heart unexpectedly light. "Come, come, Tattercoats, my dear, of course I understand. But we had better lace you into your finery, for you will dance the galliard tonight with Lord Gallimaufry before the Queen herself!"

Tattercoats laughed and clapped her hands, her tears and fears forgotten. "Oh, Malkin, Malkin, do you think so? Oh, it will be fine indeed to see the Queen! And to . . . to dance the galliard too." And then she blushed and looked away.

So Malkin was able to call the maid and ask her to dress the Lady in her fine clothes, then go in search of Pug down the winding polished stairs of the mansion. It smelled good, this house—of beeswax and comfits and roses. The open windows let in light evening air and the smell of herbs from the knotted gardens below. There were painted cloths on the walls, depicting famous scenes of classical fame: the doomed lovers Pyramus and Thisbe, whispering through their wall; the crowned Diana leaping through the forest with her hunters; the Amazon warrior queen Hippolyta, her arrow pointing at the heart of the selfish Theseus; and more, many more. They were beautiful, even moving scenes. Malkin was waylaid for quite a while by the painted plays, and it was when she was examining the last of them that she became aware of Pug's light presence near her.

"They are lovely, aren't they?" she murmured, and he shrugged.

"Pretty enough . . ."

"Look here," she said, peering at the very last picture, a scene set in some great woods. "This is a lovely one, Pug. But strange too. There's a man with a donkey's head, lying in that lovely woman's lap! What a silly smile he's got. No wonder! And look—little creatures flitting around him, bringing him . . . a drink, is it, Pug? And look, in the shadows beyond them, a man who looks like a king, watching. And look! Someone with him, with pointy ears . . . someone who looks familiar. Now, who is it? It looks just like . . ."

"Who cares," said Pug. "These people paint what they want."

She looked up at his cross tone and smiled. "I believe you don't know, Pug!" She reached out a hand to ruffle his thick hair, but he ducked, and as he did so, the heavy locks fell away from his face, and for the first time she saw his ears. She stared. Pointed ears, just like . . . Her eyes darted to the painting, then back to her friend. "Pug!" she called, as the gooseherd went off down the corridor, dancing to the tune of his own pipe. "Come back, come back! I have a question to ask you!"

≫ ≫ ≪ ≪

Despite his limp she didn't catch up with him until she reached the garden. Then she found she could no longer remember her question, as if it had been spirited away from her mind. Or perhaps it didn't matter anymore, which is possibly the same thing. Instead, she said: "Pug, Pug, I did so want to go to the ball too! Why can't I?"

He took his mouth away from the reed. "Of course you can, of course you may," he said.

"But . . ." She looked down at herself, at her lovely yet earthbound clothes. Then she said, in a rush: "Oh, Pug, I would so much have liked to wear the other dress. You know, the feather dress . . ."

"Of course you can, of course you may," he said again, his eyes twinkling.

"But . . . we left it behind . . ."

"What is that you wear around your neck?" he said, in a bewildering change of subject. "Oh, my heart, look, for it is a heart, and hearts are made to be broken!"

Her hand went to her neck automatically. But still she did not understand, until he reached out to her and, with a light, cool finger, touched a spring in the heart locket. It divided, and Malkin, too taken by surprise to move, saw deep within it a shimmer of softness, a thread of glitter. She pulled at the thread, and it unwound and came spiraling out of the locket, faster and faster, until at her feet lay a wash of shimmering gleams of color: the feather dress, beside which the silver and grape-skin marvel in Tattercoats's room looked like the silver paper of a Maying queen. She stared again into the depths of her locket and saw three more threads. In a dream she pulled at them, and there they were, the soft grass shoes, beside which Tattercoats's silver-gilt slippers seemed heavy and cold, and the cap of deep green velvet, beside which the carcanet looked like the tawdry tinsel of a Christmas play. She put on the cap, and put up a hand to stroke it gently. As she did so, she felt a tingle under her fingers, a tingle that felt almost alive, a buzz of magic that warmed her to her toes.

"They were kept warm over your heart, in your heart of gold," Pug whispered, as Malkin gazed at him in wonder and joy.

Then she was on her knees on the grass, in billows of feathered fabric.

At last she looked up at him and smiled. "I will go to the court in these," she said.

"Why not?" said Pug, as if it hadn't all been his doing. Then he added, "But you will have to go without me, for I am not one for such things."

"Oh, Pug!" she said, suddenly dismayed. "But . . ."

"But nothing," he said firmly. "You do not need me. You must not need me, for you must follow your own path." He came very close and looked deep into her eyes for a moment. "All you need are your eyes, wide open; your ears, flapping. If, after all, you should want to see me, there is your cap. But it may not help overmuch. Remember, above all, to trust your heart." He smiled. "But there is no need for fear, my friend, my Lady Malkin." And he began playing his reed again, and as he played, Malkin's heart filled with a light golden happiness that made her feel as though she might float away.

» Fifteen «

They were laughing again as the coach turned down the Strand and toward the palace. It was as though the sweetest of music was in their ears, the lightest, fizziest wine was in their veins, and everything was turning their hearts over. They had marveled at one another's transformation, looked at one another in delight: Gallimaufry in his kingfisher blue and gold, Tabor in black velvet and white lace, Tattercoats in her grape-skin and silver, and Pennyroyal in russet and black brocade, her belt hung with miniature jeweled perfume bottles.

Malkin, the others said, wore a very fine dress of pearl and mist-colored silk. A kind of veil seemed to hang over their eyes, as if they truly could not see the feather dress. Malkin wondered at this, though she had more than half-expected it because of Tattercoats's first reaction to the dress and the way the others had seen not coins but leaves. Obviously this was a part of the glamour wrought by Pug—that she was to see some of the things denied to the others. The vague pictures, without form or outline, that had been in her head since they left Fisher Forest had begun to solidify in her mind, but did not quite make sense. Yet they would soon, she knew. She did not touch her cap—not yet.

At last Pennyroyal stopped laughing and said, a little more seriously: "We have forgotten one thing, my lords and ladies. We must smell sweet for our appearance at court." She did not wait for their answers, but began busily unscrewing the gorgeous glass stoppers of her tiny bottles. "Here, for you, Tabor, is strawberry essence, for one independent and combative of spirit; and here, Malkin, gold fernseed ointment for one who sees much with heart and mind; and here, Tattercoats, the ambergold and love-in-idleness-no-more that I promised you . . . Ah! Wormwood and withers take it!" She had knocked a splash of the gold and scarlet last-named liquid onto Gallimaufry's hand. "Oh, no matter. There . . . Now, for you, Gallimaufry, here is sweet sorrel, for you are a sweet musician indeed, and everything you say is music—to one lady's ears anyway!"

She looked up and smiled at the lovers' confusion. "For myself, vanilla, for I am plain and homely yet have remained longer on the earth than any of you.' Tis a pity our friend the gooseherd is not with us, for I had some perfect concoction for him." She sat back, puffing a little but well satisfied. "There! We will not disgrace any court, for I warrant we will smell as good as any there!"

The carriage was full of the sweet smells of garden and kitchen and meadow, and unexpectedly Malkin felt as if Pug was there. She could almost hear his pipe.

"As Pennyroyal has given us such a gift, it is now my turn," said Gallimaufry gravely. Malkin noticed his hand still lay lightly on Tattercoats's. "A song, a song, to take us to court . . ."

With sorrel and silver and smiles we bless you;
With dreams of splendor we bid you come.
Yet something more lovely, and given to few,
Awaits fair and rich, awaits us some:
And I bid you good evening, good day and good night:
Good night to the evening, good day to the light.

"That is a senseless song!" said Tabor, even as Tattercoats smiled at Gallimaufry. "Here is my gift."

He beat his palms one against the other, drumming without a drum, the hard horniness of his hands booming almost like drumskin. It was a strange and stirring sound that filled every corner of the carriage and the air around. *Boom, bang, boom,* like the beating of a heart, like the footsteps of fate. *Boom, boom, boom . . .*

Then there they were! The coachman had drawn up within a great arc of buildings that stretched through acres of pleasant green. Whitehall, or Westminster Palace as it was also called, was no grand pile but rather a splendid village, with its medley of buildings. The London-Westminster highway passed through it, under two gatehouses that had been designed by a great artist in the Queen's father's day. On the west side was the tiltyard, where the Queen and her court might watch the tournaments that were still held, and the cockpit and bearyard, where fierce fights to the death between animals were watched, as well as the many lodgings of grandees and lords. On the east side, which swept down to the river, were the Queen's private garden, chapel, and state apartments, including the great hall, where the party was to be held, and the presence chamber, where they would all have to go first to be introduced to the Queen. The Queen did not normally spend the summer in Whitehall, but on special occasions she and her retinue might return to London from Nonsuch or Greenwich or wherever she was, to attend just such an occasion.

They were here, at journey's end. Their hearts were in their mouths as each in turn stepped down from the carriage onto the cobbles of a very busy courtyard. Pennyroyal said, in a whisper to Malkin, "I have read much about the court, but never did I think to find myself here!"

Malkin was too overcome to speak. Could she pass muster here? Unlike Tattercoats, she was not to the manor born. She put a hand to her head, nervously straightening her cap, and as she did, suddenly thought she saw Pug in a corner of the yard. He was not alone; he stood, watchfully silent and somehow different, between two others who were similar to him, in a way Malkin couldn't quite place. Then, as she stared and dropped her hand, they disappeared. She blinked and looked again, but now there was no one to be seen. A crinkle of cold crept up her spine to her head, but she said nothing, merely followed the others in Pennyroyal's billowing wake. The older woman somehow seemed possessed of a confidence and a knowledge of the court you would not have suspected. Perhaps, thought Malkin, if you read enough about something, it was as good as having been there in reality.

Pennyroyal chatted on and on. "Of course, you know the Earl of Malmsey is one of the Queen's godsons, and as she has no children of her own, he is precious to her, which is why there is going to be a grand party! And we will see the Queen in the presence chamber, but she may not stay for the whole party in the hall, though I hear she is a great dancer. Rose of Beauty! What joy to think I shall see the Queen at last! How proud I am that a woman should sit on the throne!"

Tabor said grumpily, "They do say that a country with a queen is better ruled, for it is ruled by men, while one with a king is ruled by women."

"They are wrong," said Pennyroyal fiercely. "Our Bess rules herself! Any man that thinks to rule her soon understands that!"

A man in a motley of splendidly colored silks—not, as they found out, a grand courtier as he looked but a mere servant—now took charge of them. "Welcome, my lords and ladies," he said, and soon showed that he was as gossipy and feather-tongued as Pennyroyal. He asked where they came from, not stopping to hear the answer but going on to sing London's praises. He told them breathlessly about the high entertainment that awaited them that night. "There is a Venetian come, a lord, who has some skill in conjuring and magic, and he is to show us many strange things," he said. "I expect there will be colored smoke aplenty, and much silver paper and alchemical wonders—I have seen many such!" he sighed, with a world-weary air.

Malkin glanced over at Tattercoats meaningfully, but that girl had no eyes or ears for anything but the palace and Gallimaufry at her side.

"What is this lord's name?" Malkin asked.

"He is called Count Oscuro," said the man. Then, cattily, "All Venetians are called 'Count,' and have golden hair, whether real or painted, don't you find?"

The man did not notice her reaction, for he continued chattering busily, telling them of all the grand personages who were already in the presence chamber awaiting the Queen's coming. "There's the Archbishop of Canterbury—aye—and the

Bishop of London, a great number of State counselors, and officers of the crown, and gentlemen, and ladies! Come quickly, for soon there will be no place to stand. You will want to be announced to the gentlemen who introduces lords and ladies to the Queen. What names shall I give him?"

By now they had come through the corridors to the presence chamber itself. An immense scented heat flowed out from its doors, so crowded was it, so full of color both from the courtiers' clothes and the rich tapestries on the walls, and so redolent of a hundred, no, two hundred fragrances, and of bodily sweats and the fresh dry smell of the hay that had been strewn on the floor before the Queen's coming. The servant turned to them again. "Now, what names?"

They gazed at one another, panic-stricken. Then Tattercoats said in her soft voice: "Tell him to announce the Lady Susanna de Montacour, granddaughter of the Baron of Fisher Forest. And my friends: Sir Galli de Maufry, and the Marquis of Tabor from France, the Lady Penelope Royell, and my dearest cousin, Lady Malkin."

Malkin stood as if turned to stone, her eyes stinging, her heart full. The others all looked at one another, smiling. Who would have thought such invention could exist in Tattercoats's gentle head? The servant bowed. "At your service," he said, and then left them, heading through the crowd toward a most distinguished-looking gentleman in velvet who stood at the far door.

Then, quite suddenly, came a stir, a hush, and then a blast of trumpets. Everyone in the room crowded back, leaving a passage in the middle of the room as the Queen's cortege advanced from the far door. First came gentlemen, knights, barons, earls, and such, all richly dressed, with no hats on their heads; then came the Chancellor, carrying the royal seals in a red silk purse, and flanked by two gentlemen, one carrying the royal sceptre, the other the sword of state in a rich red scabbard studded with golden fleur-de-lis.

"The emblem of both Royal France and Royal England," Tabor whispered excitedly to Malkin, who hardly heard. For there now was the Queen. She was middling tall, and hardly showed her age at all, her gaze steady, her fair skin only a little wrinkled. Her very red hair was piled up on her head, a small crown resting on the very top. She had pearl drops in her small ears and a magnificent pearl necklace. Her dress was of white silk set with pearls the size of beans, and over that she wore a mantle of black silk shot with silver threads. Her long train was carried by one of her ladies, and many more ladies followed, mostly dressed in white. By her side was the gentleman whose birthday it was today, and whom the Queen had honored with her unusual summer presence at her winter palace: the Earl of Malmsey. He was tall and fair, with dark eyes, a curling moustache and beard, and dressed gorgeously in red and white silks and velvet.

Malkin tried to catch Tattercoats's eye, but the girl was resolutely looking at the Queen and not at the Queen's godson. As the Queen advanced, flanked by the Earl and the important-looking gentleman in velvet, she stopped to speak to this person and that, each time smiling graciously. As she got closer, Malkin heard her speaking first in English, then switching to some other language, and thought admiringly of how she must know all the languages of the world. The Earl looked on with an expressionless face; the velvet gentleman whispered in the Queen's ear occasionally, no doubt telling her who this or that one was, and the Queen tilted her head toward them and spoke briefly in her low, pleasant voice while they bowed or curtsied, and then she passed on.

At last she came to our friends, and the gentleman whispered in her ear. In her nervousness Malkin's hand fluttered at the heart locket on her throat. Then she dropped it as if she had been scalded, for she heard Pug's voice, gay and jaunty, whispering: "This is not my Queen. My Queen is elsewhere. Look with your eyes and your ears and your heart, Malkin, my sweet, for soon you will need them more than you think."

In the instant she heard the voice, and before it faded away, she caught sight, over the Queen's left shoulder, of a familiar violet gaze, piercing her where she stood. As a result she hardly heard the Queen's pleasant murmur, hardly saw Elizabeth's fine, deep-gray gaze. Then the Queen had passed on, and Malkin was left knowing her moment of history had been made, and she had missed it, pierced to the heart by the disturbing gaze of a magician's eyes.

» Sixteen «

The court swept all around them in a colored flood, and Malkin, caught in its eddies, lost sight of her friends. She tried to catch up, but the crowd was too large, too noisy, and too bright for her to be able to distinguish anyone in particular. She could not see Oscuro either, and these two facts together made her feel uneasy. Yet, after all, Oscuro so far had done nothing. There was only an uneasy feeling to accuse him with, and that would not stand up in any court at all, save perhaps that of the heart.

"Where are we going?" she said at last, addressing a young woman near her.

The woman looked at her incredulously. "We are off to the banqueting house, of course, for the entertainment." She turned back to her companion, obviously not wishing to be further associated with a provincial ignoramus.

Malkin was none the wiser; she had no idea what a banqueting house was. It sounded like a place where you ate, though; she hoped so, for she was hungry now. She followed the crowd in silence, listening to the scraps of conversation around her. Once or twice she heard the name of the Earl of Malmsey, spoken in none too nattering a way. It sounded like the Queen's godson had few friends among the courtiers. Malkin thought of the figure she had seen walking by the Queen. He had seemed handsome in a blank sort of way—the dark eyes had given nothing away. Being close to power always makes others envious, she thought. It did not mean that there was anything wrong with the Earl.

The banqueting house was a very large wooden structure with canvas sides painted to look like stone. The crowd milled around excitedly, and Malkin now noticed that it had grown very much larger. Obviously the entertainment was open to more than just the court, for there were people from the city too. In the crush it was impossible to see Tattercoats or the others, and Malkin felt a flutter of panic in her chest. People behind her were pressing close. She wondered briefly if there were nips and hoists here, ready to cut purses or pick pockets, and decided that if there weren't, it would be a miracle indeed. But that would not concern her—she had nothing on her to steal except for the small amount of gold left in her pouch, and she had the notion that anyone who stole that would get a nasty surprise, as the boatman had.

Inside the banqueting house, hundreds of glass lamps sent ricochets of golden light in all directions, illuminating the tiered steps where people would sit or stand; the stage, with its canvas screens painted with clouds and starry skies and suns; and the flowers and fruit and other plants made of canvas and wicker, spangled with gold, hanging from the roofs and the sides of the hall. It was a place that stilled all Malkin's fears and doubts, a place of enchantment and happiness, though there was no sign of food anywhere. She only wished she could be with her friends, to see Tattercoats's joy and the others' wonder.

"A most interesting place, is it not?" The voice by her side was silky, amused.

Malkin turned.

The violet eyes regarded her calmly, without any surprise. "I have been wanting to speak to you for some time," Oscuro said. He bowed.

"I am not important," Malkin said, her throat thickening, her heart hammering. How did he know her, in these new clothes? Why was he watching her with that smile? The questions beat in her brain, but she forced herself to speak as calmly as he. "Why should you wish to speak to me?"

Oscuro smiled. "Come, come. Let us not waste time, my dear Malkin. I know who you are; you know who I am. But you do not realize we both want the same thing: Tattercoats's happiness and the old lord's peace of mind. That is all I have been contracted to do. There was no need to run away, Malkin." His accent was soft, the stress on her name gentle. It disturbed her strangely.

"You have no need of me," Malkin snapped. She looked desperately over the heads of the crowd, trying to glimpse the flame of Tattercoats's hair. "I am only a servant. And your contract is intended to bleed money from the old lord, to offer him false hope. It has nothing to do with my Lady Susanna."

Oscuro smiled again. "A servant? Here? Dressed in such splendid mist-silver taffeta, like a great lady?" (So, he did not see her in her true clothes either. Somehow the knowledge gave Malkin heart.) "Come, Malkin, do not play with me. And besides, you misunderstand me. I do not offer the old lord false hope. I offer him the real hope of his granddaughter. If you had not run away, you would have seen that. You and I, Malkin, we want the same thing. If . . . the Lady Susanna marries the Earl of Malmsey, then all will be well. For the old lord has come to understand that his daughter cannot return, but that her daughter can warm his old heart because of her resemblance to her mother, and that an alliance with the house of Malmsey will restore to him the power and the illustriousness he once had. You see, when his daughter, Margaret, was young, the Baron was one of the leading lights of the court. Indeed, the Queen herself stayed at Fisher Forest once. And before Margaret married Will de Montacour, she had another suitor—a mysterious one, but certainly a lord of great power. The Baron never knew for sure, he never met him, but he had a strong suspicion from his daughter's hints that he may even have been . . ." here Oscuro looked around him, then lowered his voice to a whisper, "may even have been of *royal* blood. His daughter refused to say. But one day it all ended, no one knows why. And then she met the Montacour man. But here's a business—for I am almost certain she was already with child when she married him!"

Malkin stared at him. "How do you know this? I have never heard a whisper of it!"

"You have not traveled very far, Malkin," said Oscuro, smiling. "I have heard things in all sorts of places. Let us say . . . I have reliable information."

"But . . . the Queen has no sons. It could not be . . ."

"No, no, not sons. But a cousin perhaps. Or even a foreign prince of the blood royal. The fact is that for quite some time after that—before the Lady Susanna's birth and her mother's death—there were distinct but discreet signs of royal patronage: mysterious parcels of gold and jewels, great good fortune for all the family."

Malkin shrugged. "Why are you telling me this?" she said coldly. "It is a ridiculous, unbelievable story. More false hopes to plant in the old lord's head. Will de Montacour is my friend's father."

"I am telling you," said Oscuro tensely, "because it is important. So that you will trust me. I am telling you the truth. Ignore it at your peril. If de Montacour was really your friend's father, why did he abandon her?"

Malkin retorted: "Why then did the Baron abandon his granddaughter, refuse to see her? It makes no sense, Oscuro."

"Because," said the magician triumphantly, "when his daughter died, the patronage ceased. Ill luck dogged him, grief unhinged him. But now he is ready to begin again. I have not given him false hopes, Malkin, but a way out of his self-imposed exile. And, incidentally, a new life for his granddaughter. A marriage alliance with the Earl of Malmsey would be a brilliant comeback."

Malkin's heart beat wildly. "But why should the Earl want that?"

"If the Earl knows of Susanna's real parentage . . ." Oscuro looked thoughtfully out over the crowd, as if seeking out the Earl's golden head, "he will understand at once the advantage. The Queen has no heirs, except for that son of her Scottish cousin's. How much better it would be if . . ."

Malkin stared at him, her face paling. She knew that such speculation could lead one to the Tower, and to the gallows. She said: "This is all wild talk, with no basis in anything. It explains nothing and confuses everything. Truly the work of an Italian."

Oscuro smiled, and this time his eyes stayed cold. "Malkin, I am warning you. You and I have much in common. Together we can do much—if only you are willing to see, to really see and understand. But if you are not with me, then you must be against me. And in that case, know that my powers are as great as yours, and probably much greater!" With a swirl of his silk cloak, he strode away from her, threading through the lines of people as if he knew exactly where he was going.

Malkin stayed where she was until she was elbowed by an impatient woman behind her and told to keep moving or she would not get a place to stand. She wanted to shout after Oscuro: "No, no, no, I have nothing in common with you. I neither need nor want an alliance with you!" But the brave words had no real echo in her deepest heart, which remembered that from the start Oscuro had disturbed her strangely, as if she recognized something in him—something she recognized in herself too. He was not telling her everything, she was sure of it; something was being kept back. But was he telling the truth at all, about Tattercoats's parentage? She could scarcely credit it, and perhaps it was merely the mystification of a liar and a cheat, a marvelous way of weaseling into the good graces and the capacious purse of the Baron, and perhaps that of the Earl too. A whispered royal connection would do Tattercoats's prospects as a bride no harm, though it could also place her in very great danger from the courtiers and even the Queen herself. Would one who was the Queen's godson, and as such, surely loyal and loving, want any hand in such a dubious enterprise? Still, there were those things she had overheard about the Earl . . . and none of them had sounded very flattering.

On the other hand, such a connection could explain why Tattercoats would be helped to go to the ball, to come back into her true inheritance. . . . But if that were so, why would Pug have a hand in it? And what had become of that first, so-called royal, suitor? Why had he not protected his supposed child? Oh, Malkin thought, head spinning, I wish Pug were here! That was another strange thing—Oscuro had not mentioned Pug at all. Why not, when it was Pug's powers that were great, not Malkin's. He seemed to ascribe far too great an importance to her, who was merely Tattercoats's friend. Had she been wrong in fearing Oscuro? And if she had, what did it mean? What was

Pug's part in all this? Could it be that *he* was the one she should have feared instead? What was Pug's real motive, then?

There were no answers, none at all, in her head, which was dizzied by the confusions whirling around in it. She clutched distractedly at her hair, and as she did so, two things happened: a loud drum roll filled the air, heralding the start of the entertainment, and she saw Pug standing at the other side of the room from her, his face grave and still, even unfriendly.

» Seventeen «

First there were dances, and a sort of play between a man done up as a savage, and a woman—or dressed-up boy—as Echo, a nymph answering him. At the end of the play, a shower of painted stars and flowers fell from the ceiling, and everyone clapped. Then there was an interval, and servants passed among the crowd with trays of food. Malkin should have been pleased by that, but her hunger had almost vanished, so that she only nibbled absently. She tried to push through the crowd to find her friends, or even Oscuro, but there was no sign of either. She had not found Pug. By now she had realized that he was only visible when she touched her cap of moss-velvet, and she was not in a hurry to touch that again. She did not want to see the unfriendly set of Pug's face, even though her heart grieved for sight of him. He would know what to do. Oscuro was wrong, quite wrong: it was not she who had power, it was Pug.

The Earl of Malmsey was standing a little to one side, away from the people pressing respectfully about his godmother. Closer up, the blankness of his gaze seemed more like wariness. The perfect mask of his face owed something to artifice, a spot of powder or paint perhaps. A man in such a position had a heavy burden, for he could never truly say what he thought or felt. Perhaps in private . . . perhaps. He must know that people thought him too handsome, untrustworthy, sly, depending on a doting old woman, as Malkin had heard whispered; all this and more. As Malkin watched him, he looked up and suddenly caught her gaze. His eyes were very dark brown, almost black, and long-lashed: nightflower eyes that would tell you very little. He narrowed his gaze a little, and a smile curled about his lips. Malkin felt a small bounding of her heart as she realized the Earl was looking at her *appraisingly*, as if she were a lady he wanted to *know* better. She dropped her eyes and moved rapidly away, but was aware still of his gaze. She guessed that those eyes did not forget a face, once seen, and told herself, vainly, that she did not care.

The entertainment began again. A sweating, fat player bellowed: "You are now about to witness the most excellent silent play of how the great magician Oscuro the Obscure came to the fairy kingdom of Aureola and Auberon, where nothing is as it seems to be! Watch, ladies and gentlemen, masters and mistresses, and you will see sights of glamour and magic!"

As he finished speaking, a golden sedan chair constructed of paper and wicker came into the hall, held on the shoulders of four very small men, who were all clothed in spangles and sparkles, their faces powdered with some gilded stuff. In the sedan chair sat a figure dressed in long sparkly robes, a crown of glitter on her head. The crowd hushed a little as the sedan chair stopped and the figure stepped onto the stage. This must be Queen Aureola.

Malkin, watching intently, fiddled at her throat, brushing the golden locket. Immediately she heard Pug's voice, hissing: "See how they think they know us, Malkin! Watch, Malkin. Watch!"

She dropped her hand quickly. She was tired of cryptic instructions and riddles without answers. The figure on the stage was now walking, hands wringing, long robes trailing. Then all at once, from one corner of the stage came another figure draped in a long cloak, wearing a golden mask in the shape of a hawk's head. She knew it was Oscuro even before she saw the brilliant blond of his hair.

A swirl of the cloak, a flourish of gestures, then suddenly in the magician's hand, where certainly nothing had been before, a beautiful glass ball, which he handed to the fairy queen with much bowing. She mimed delight, then took the ball, looked deep into it, and mimed distress. At that moment, from another corner of the stage strode a man as small as the bearers, but wearing a gold paper crown. The fairy king. Oscuro turned to him, his hands fluttering again, and there was a bird in his cupped palm—a beautiful small bird, a robin with a flaming red breast, which flew onto his shoulder and trilled sweetly. The crowd gasped and Oscuro bowed. But just as he turned back to the fairy monarchs, the Queen stamped her foot. And suddenly there on her wrist was another bird. It was a big bird, a raven, glossy and black, with beady bright eyes, and it looked at the cowering robin and gave a loud, croaking cry. Malkin felt that cry like a dagger going into her flesh, and hardly noticed the delight-ed applause of the crowd or the way both robin and raven dis-appeared with practiced ease back into the folds of the actors' clothing. A memory had surged up into her mind, something conjured by the mime she had just seen, something just on the edge of consciousness. She couldn't quite grab hold of it, but the mere fleetingness of it left a trail of distress in her mind. Tatter-coats! Where was Tattercoats? Somehow it seemed urgent to find her.

But in the very next instant, she caught sight of Tattercoats's bright hair, close to that of the Earl of Malmsey, who bent over her hand. Her heart stopped pounding, and she told herself sternly that she had been imagining a meaning where there was only well-worn sleight of hand. There it is. What I wanted for her will be accomplished. The Earl of Malmsey will be delighted with her, she thought, and strangely, her heart felt like it would break. She looked for Gallimaufry, but could not see him or the other two.

A long, drawn-out sigh from the crowd brought her atten-tion back to the stage. From Oscuro's hands issued a trickle, a stream, a river, a lake of colored smoke that billowed faster and faster, filling first the stage—hiding the king, the queen, the bear-ers, the sedan chair, the magician—and then flowing out into the rest of the hall. The smoke seemed to make patterns and shapes. Within it she thought she could see all manner of agitating things. And the smoke grew so dense that you could not see anything; but then, just as quickly, it cleared away, like mist com-ing off a mirror.

There was Oscuro on the stage, bowing, and the fairy king and queen. The sweating fat man came up onto the stage again and bellowed, "We have come to an end. Midsummer's bonfires are outside, ladies and gentlemen! Meanwhile, God save our Queen!"

The room erupted with "God save the Queen!" A low, pleasant voice was heard saying, "I thank you, my people," and there was a rustle as the Queen's party prepared to go.

>> >> << <<

The Earl of Malmsey had not followed his godmother out. It was his birthday, of course; he would revel for a while yet. Malkin saw his straight figure some distance from her, but no Tattercoats beside him. She looked for her friend's flame-colored hair, but it had been swallowed up again in the crowd. Perhaps it was time for her too to go, though where to she had no idea. Would the coach be waiting for her outside?

"There you are, Malkin." Pennyroyal was by her side, smiling with what looked like relief. "I thought we had lost you for good." She sighed. "My feet are hurting so. I do not like these stiff shoes." She shuffled her feet a little. "I should like to be sitting by the side of a stream right now, Malkin, an apronful of simples gathered, looking forward to distilling next day!" She peered at Malkin. "Why, what's the matter, my dear? You do not look yourself."

"There is nothing wrong with me," Malkin began stiffly. Then she relented. "I am sorry. I am simply tired. Weary. Bone-aching."

Pennyroyal looked at her shrewdly. "My dear, I know what ails you." She fumbled at her belt. "Some more perfume . . ."

But Malkin had seen Gallimaufry. To her utter amazement, he was at the center of an admiring ring of ladies, his voice rising and falling, his hands gesturing, his smile flashing. She looked back at Pennyroyal. "What ails me is that we all seem to forget our hearts."

Pennyroyal shrugged. "Yonder Marquis of Motley cannot help his nature," she said. "But he loves my Lady true."

Here now was Tabor, smiling. "The bonfires are lit," he said. "Quick, come with me, I must see if these English fires are as good as those we make on Saint John's Eve!" He grinned.

"Much better!" said Pennyroyal indignantly, but to Malkin's surprise she took the arm he offered and sailed regally out with him. Gallimaufry broke away from his admiration society and came toward Malkin.

"Come, Malkin, do not look so glum! It's Midsummer's Eve!" Then he frowned a little. "But where is my Lady? We were to meet for the bonfires, after the boring Earl had relieved her of his company. He has done so; I saw him alone a short while ago, though I can't see him now. Is she not with you?"

"You can see she is not," snapped Malkin.

Gallimaufry shrugged. "She must have already gone to the bonfires." His tone was jaunty, but Malkin saw that his eyes were not. He thinks she has gone somewhere with the Earl, Malkin said to herself. And that somewhere outside on this midsummer's night, the love of his heart is being lost to another. Why doesn't he just rush out and look for her? Of course, it must be because he thinks he has no right. He believes the dream is ending and soon he will find himself on the road again, a ragged man in ragged clothes, living off his wits, while Tattercoats—Susanna—is a real baron's granddaughter who will soon forget her humble friends, as if they had been just a dream too.

"Come with me," Malkin said firmly. "We will go and seek her."

≫ ≫ ≪ ≪

The night was red and black and golden from the huge bonfires that leapt crackling into the air, and filled with the strong smells of the burning wood. Sparks flew in the air, the flames licked brightly, strange shadows capered about them: people elongated, flattened, and changed by the playlight of the flames. There was laughter and singing and clapping, with almost as much excitement as if this were a village festival. Midsummer, midyear, midnight. At this time everything lay open. It was a time of great joy and great unease too, for anything could happen in a time that was neither one thing nor the other.

Gallimaufry and Malkin searched and searched for Tatter-coats. They found Pennyroyal and Tabor, and they searched too. They saw the Earl of Malmsey several times, then not at all. Malkin saw Oscuro once, and even the Baron once, but of Tattercoats there was not a sign. Not a whisper. Not a look.

» Eighteen «

It was not until dawn that the companions found a clue to Tattercoats's disappearance, and it was from an unexpected source. One of the courtiers, rather the worse for wear, was sprawled under a tree in the park, his head on the lap of his lady love. Wearily Malkin put her question to him, a question it seemed she had asked close to a hundred times: "We are looking for the Lady Susanna de Montacour. She has hair the color of flame and is wearing a dress the color of grape-skin and silver. Have you seen her?"

The courtier—a well-built man with handsome, but rather dissolute features—glanced up at them and laughed. His lady laughed too, more decorously, and kept stroking his long, curly black hair as if she were petting a cat. When he had stopped laughing, the man said: "Hair the color of flame! Dress the color of grape-skin and silver! You paint a fine picture, my Lady!"

Malkin turned away. She was in no mood for the foolishness of a drunk.

Then he said, still hiccuping with laughter, "But then, we may have seen such a one as you describe." He took a long draught from his cup and smiled up at his woman. "Perchance we have, is that not so, my Lady?"

She nodded wisely, and winked. "Perchance." Glancing coquettishly but a trifle vaguely at Gallimaufry, she murmured, *"Susanna fair, oh Susanna fair . . ."*

Gallimaufry smiled back reluctantly. "A most beautiful song indeed," he murmured, "by the greatest of English songbirds. Malkin, do you know it? It goes like this . . ."

Even in such an extremity, the musician in him takes precedence, thought Malkin sourly. Pennyroyal, with a shrewd look at

101

the others, interrupted him. "Well, my Lord, we are indeed grateful for your help. It is plain, however, that you have much to occupy you. We will be on our way."

"Stay, stay," said the courtier, suddenly sulky. "I did not tell all."

"No, he did not tell all," said his lady indignantly.

Her support seemed to lend new strength to her suitor's arm, new clarity to his brain, for he struggled to sit up. With some dignity he attempted to quell the spirituous enemy within that had already breached his walls. "I saw her some time ago, going toward the . . . the highway. Highway to the city. There was a man with her, and a coach waiting. A black coach." He fell back again and did not speak for a while.

His lady repeated proudly, "A black coach, he says. A *black* coach," with a witless emphasis on the color that made Malkin want to strangle her.

The courtier opened one eye, an eye that had practically lost its fight to focus, and said, with the hiccuping laughter back in his voice, "She went not so willingly, oh yes! And the man—he was huge, hunched, all in black, cloaked. Like a great black raven, yes, and her so small, her hair red, as you say."

"Like a great black raven," the lady enunciated carefully, beaming. "Do you hear?"

"A robin taken by a raven," the man laughed. "*Susanna fair* . . ." he started to sing, his voice surprisingly thin and wispy. Not another word could they get out of him or his lady, who had joined in the song in a quavering two-part cacophony that would have made the composer banish them to the ends of the Earth if he had heard it.

≫ ≫ ≪ ≪

"It's the Baron, it must be the Baron! And Oscuro must have a hand in this!" Gallimaufry was raging. "Wait till I get them! I will skewer them with cutting words, I will nail them to ferocious deeds!"

"They will feel the bite of my rapier, those ruffians!" said Tabor wildly, thumping the hilt of his sword. "They will see what a man of King Henri can do!"

"But, my dears," said Pennyroyal gently, "what good will that do? We must find our Tattercoats first."

She looked in appeal to Malkin, who nodded absently. The courtier's words had sent unaccountable tremors through her. The image of the great black raven hunched over the cowering Tattercoats filled her with almost unbearable terror and grief. She remembered Oscuro's conjuring, the birds in his play, and shivered. She remembered his warning earlier, remembered the Baron's black coach, remembered their own flight from Fisher Forest. Perhaps that's where they'd take Tattercoats. But why? Surely their aim was to get Tattercoats betrothed to the Earl of Malmsey? Why, then, take her away? Unless . . . She remembered the stories about Oscuro, about how he had fled Italy, a poisoner, a murderer, a dangerous person altogether. Who knew what dark and devious devices lurked in the Italian's mind?

"We must go," she said at last, not even aware that the others were still arguing among themselves. "We must follow them."

"Follow?" said Gallimaufry.

"Follow them to the city, of course," said Tabor crossly.

That is where the Baron has taken her?" said Pennyroyal.

"No, of course not," said Gallimaufry self-importantly. "Further than the city, of course. He has taken her . . . taken her to wherever it is that ravens go."

"To Fisher Forest," said Tabor triumphantly. "A bird always returns to its own nest."

"However foul," agreed Pennyroyal, nodding her head. She glanced at the others, raised her eyebrows, and said clearly and loudly, as if she were speaking to a person who was hard of hearing, "So, Mistress Malkin, are we bound thither?"

"A raven . . ." Malkin murmured. "A raven . . . now why do I . . . ?" She gazed wildly at her expectant friends and clutched at her heart locket. She almost reeled back at the wave of longing and grief that filled her then. A moment later the locket went cold and blank, became once more just gilded metal lying against her skin. Her eyes smarting with tears, she said harshly: "Nothing. It is not important. But Tabor is right. We must retrace our steps, go back to Fisher Forest."

"Where is our coach?" said Gallimaufry. "We must find it and tell the coachman to make for the forest as fast as possible!"

Malkin shook her head. "We have no coach, Gallimaufry," she said sadly. To herself she whispered, "We are no longer under the kind eye of the Other Country." She touched her cap of rushes and saw no visions, no Pug, no help to be had. "We must go, though, and quickly, before . . . before . . ." She set out at a run, through the trees, toward the highway. After a startled moment, the others set out after her. And not a moment too soon.

Just as they emerged from the palace grounds and set foot on the dirt of the road, their splendid clothes vanished. They were once more a bunch of ragged rogues and vagabonds, liable to be locked up by smug London watchdogs, and certainly not welcome at court. Only the cold metal of the locket, now deaf and dumb against Malkin's skin, remained of her finery. The others, it seemed, had been left with nothing to remember it by.

» Nineteen «

It was a sad and sorry little party that made its footsore way down the same road they had whisked along so gaily on their way to the palace. Nobody spoke, not even to remark on Pug's absence. But then he had not been with them at court, and they had not remarked on that either, thought Malkin dispiritedly. As long as someone led them, told them what to do. . . . Her first urgency was slowly being replaced by a terrible weariness.

The sun was now well and truly up, though sulking beneath a blanket of clouds. The road was already busy: people hurrying on as if the good fortune of the world lay under the soles of their bustling feet; merchants and salespeople of all kinds full-throatedly crying their wares as if the clamor of their marketing song could reach to the very heavens and tempt the sun from his grouchy drowsiness.

"We'll have to hire us a boat," Pennyroyal said at last, as they dragged themselves without pleasure through the streets they had looked on with such naive joy just a short time ago. Short! Why, how long ago it seemed! Time had been imprisoned by the spell of Pug, but now it was on its impatient way, quickly, huffing, puffing, crying hurry hurry hurry!

So they walked through Southwark and down to the pier. There were a few boatmen waiting, but they all turned their backs on such ragged, nonprospective customers. These London boatmen, Malkin thought, would all want to see the color of your money before they took you on, unless you had a pawned-kingdom's worth of fine clothes on your back. And there was no Pug this time to help them with gold that vanished when you looked at it too closely.

Then Malkin suddenly saw a familiar face, remembered the fistful of leaves, and shivered. She was about to call out to the others to walk down to the next pier, when . . .

"Good morning, masters, mistresses!" It was said with a villainous grin and a cocked eye by the boatman who had brought them down the river. He looked at them with a grimacing glare. "So you are off eastward, my fine friends?" His voice rasped loudly, and he took a step toward them. Beside him, the other boatmen looked up from their conversations and almost imperceptibly moved closer, as if they were about to watch a good play, or perhaps a good fight.

Tabor put a hand to his side, where no longer smart rapier but battered blade was hanging. Gallimaufry's mouth opened, no doubt on the beginnings of some complicated Erse curse. Malkin's heart fluttered like an imprisoned bird, but it was Pennyroyal who said, soothingly: "Eastward, yes, my dear boy! But stay. I do hear your poor throat has lodged some grit in its soul. Wait." She rummaged in the wooden chest that had been restored to her together with all her former tattered lack of glory. While the others watched, struck into helpless silence, she fussed and bothered until she pulled out a little silvery vial, glittering in the pale morning. "Root of soothwort," she announced briskly. "A miracle cure, my son!" She held out the little vial to the boatman, whose first reaction became suspicion in a trice. "No, *really*," she said calmly. "Try it. It does work! All my customers come back for more."

The crowd around looked interested. The boatman, however, stared at Pennyroyal, as if imprinting her features on his mind. "How do I know that it won't just turn to pitch in my throat?" He was seized with a paroxysm of coughing then that sounded as if his throat were being torn out by some wild beast.

"Oh dear, oh dear," fussed Pennyroyal. "Such a fiery throat, it could set the Thames aflame! Try my medicine, Sir. It cannot do you harm. And I *never* put pitch in my recipes," she went on, drawing herself up proudly. "It is not good for business'. Tis only good flowers and plants go into my mixtures, Sir. Of that you can be sure!"

The boatman said nothing, but his hand shot out and grabbed the silver vial by its delicate neck. He emptied the contents down his throat, with a furious glare at all and sundry. As the mixture went down his rough gullet, a remarkable transformation rippled over him. His face, which had looked so pale-surly and glaring, suddenly took on a gleaming, lordly air; his eyes, so bloodshot and full of vindictiveness, smiled like an angel's in an old church painting; and from out of his throat came a voice of such melodiousness that at first they were captivated by its sound rather than by the meaning of the words it was intoning. The transformed man said, happily: "Of course I will take you back up the river. I will be glad to! Look, my friends, the sun is shining!"

And indeed, there it was, the old grouch shaking off his tattered bedclothing and winking at them blindingly with his one brilliant eye.

The crowd dispersed, shaking its collective head, and the transformed boatman said: "Please. Come into my boat, dear friends!" He bustled, he bowed, he ushered them into his wherry as if they were truly good, even royal, friends, and they followed, very relieved but rather puzzled. Only Pennyroyal looked as if she were on firm ground. And soon she wasn't either, on account of being on the river in the boatman's swift wherry.

They were very crowded in the boat, and felt a little uneasy about how heavily it lay in the water, but the boatman took no notice. He sang and told them that now that his eyes had been opened and his throat reprieved from its pain, he would henceforward be a reformed man.

"My dear wife and my many children will bless my name," he crowed melodiously, deftly avoiding a much bigger, clumsy barge bearing down on them. "My customers will bless my skill with the oar. Oh, all will be changed, my friends!" As if in answer to his good cheer, the boat skimmed over the dark water with as much grace as a grossly overloaded wherry could muster. Malkin, remembering his racing prowess, and shifting uncomfortably on the hard bench, fervently hoped that his reformation would spread to this too. Perhaps it was merely that the boat was overloaded, but certainly the boatman was being much more careful and gentle with his charges.

Pennyroyal leaned over and whispered to Malkin: "I have never known my physics to work so quickly! Perhaps the shaking up it received in recent times helped bring this about. Or perhaps it was the vanishment of the bottles while I was in my finery. What do you think?"

"I don't know," said Malkin, though she could guess. Surely Pug had something to do with this. She shifted around a bit more. The seat really was most atrociously uncomfortable. She surreptitiously slid a hand under her dress to try to ease the pain—and encountered something hard and cold and spiky. What on earth—or rather, on water—was it? She pulled it out, and the sight of what she held struck them all dumb. A shoe. A very pretty, very hard, fashionable shoe. Made of finely chased silver so thinly spun it could have been made of Venetian glass. It was the shoe my Lady de Montacour had been wearing when last seen, or rather, one of the pair.

"That is the problem with my trade," chirped the unsurprised boatman. "People *will* leave their belongings in my wherry! Stranger things than old shoes have I seen, I can tell you!" Even the obvious magnificence of the abandoned piece of footwear did not appear to strike him unduly; his was a newly minted nature that took account only of its own gleaming leaps of happiness, not idle envy or speculation.

Malkin glared at him. Pennyroyal's brew, which had caused such a transformation in this man, was now more of a curse than a blessing, for the boatman would now not take anything seriously. She said, "When was the lady in your boat?"

"Lady?" caroled the boatman happily, as he floated his wherry in toward the bridge. "Lady? Oh, she who dropped her shoe? Careless, eh?"

In a mind-flash, Malkin saw poor Tattercoats, watched over by a hunched man like a great black raven, made to hurry, hustled along. Had she dropped her shoe without knowing it? Or had she left it as a message to her friends? If the latter, it must have been a forlorn hope, for how would she know they would take this selfsame wherry? On the other hand, if Pug was still there, somewhere, watching over them, maybe this was his way of showing them they were on the right track.

"Yes," said the boatman, smiling, "a strange couple, I thought them: him huddling her close in his great black cloak like the wings of some bird; she, flame-haired, head bent, like a fire that is quenched. I had seen her before, I thought, with other companions. Ha-ha! The world is indeed strange. But wonderful."

Malkin looked at him sharply, looking for a hint of gloating, of triumph, but his eyes, though merry, looked completely innocent of hidden meaning. He did not appear to remember the circumstances in which he had seen Tattercoats before.

By now they were at the bridge, and the boatman promised he would meet them at the other side. So they disembarked and walked quickly to the wharf below. Gallimaufry had taken charge of the shoe and had put it away sorrowfully somewhere in his motley, near his heart.

Malkin felt the sense of urgency pursuing her so quickly, like stealthy footsteps gaining inexorably, that she knew she would soon panic, run screaming as fast as she could to rescue her friend. She could not shake off the figure that crouched dimly in her mind, the raven of nightmare overshadowing the cowering robin. But she followed the others meekly enough, saying nothing of her fears and her racing pulse. If only Pug were here, with his sly smile and his sweet reed! Once, Gallimaufry said musingly, "If your gooseherd friend should appear, he would be well met indeed." But otherwise the other three made no mention of Pug's disappearance. Of course they were wandering folk, used to the uncertainties of the road, people coming and going without announcement or explanation, and had long learned not to worry or question. In the face of their calm, Malkin was too ashamed to speak of her own terrible anxiety.

Nothing further happened on the river trip, except for the ceaseless drip drip dripping of the reformed boatman's chatter. By the time they alighted, far down the Thames at a place the boatman said was near the road out of the city, Malkin was seriously wondering whether she preferred the original surly rogue.

Once they were free of his chatter and away from the noisome waterway, she felt more kindly disposed toward him. He had consented to be paid with another slim-necked vial of Pennyroyal's physic, which she named "hensteeth bane."

"A rare mixture it is too, Master Boatman," she said, wagging a finger at him . . . "so don't go wasting it!"

When they were out of his sight and hearing, she drew a deep sigh and said: "Well, I have never been able to dispose of that one. A bit of a mistake of a mixture."

The others looked at her in some dismay—would the boatman chase after them when the mixture caused him to sprout horns or a tail, or even feel a griping in his guts?

"It is harmless. I know," she insisted, to their great gales of laughter. "I know because I gave some to my cousin's hens once, as a precaution, and nothing happened!"

At last they were out of the city walls, and struggling on through the suburbs of ill repute. When they had entered the city, it had been in the splendid coach, and their feet had not touched dust or mire. But now they had to trudge through miles of it, toward the fields and woods that shimmered at what seemed a tantalizingly short distance away.

They no longer felt quite as weary as they had early in the morning; a second wind was upon them. But second winds, alas, are notoriously short of puff, and soon they would be too exhausted to even remember how to put one foot in front of the other, let alone make brisk progress of any kind. They passed thin, straggling lines of people also walking, and carters creaking along with old wagons and even older horses.

It was clear something had to be done, and it was Gallimaufry who did it for them. For some time he had been uncharacteristically quiet, his ready songs absent, his inventive lips quite silent. As they struggled up another rise and prepared to brave another nest of potholes and dust, he said: "Wait! Walk a little further and sit by the side of the road! I will catch you up shortly."

And he was off, doubling back the way they had come, light on his feet as a spring-heeled rabbit. The others obeyed; at this stage anything but walking on looked good, even squatting by dusty verges waiting for who knew what.

They did not have to wait long to find out. Along the road, at breakneck speed, came Gallimaufry—driving one of those selfsame old wagons they had passed just a short time before.

"Quick!" he gasped. "The fellow will be after us as soon as he realizes." Indeed, at that moment they heard a great shout some distance away. "Quick!" yelled Gallimaufry. "Climb on!" And without further ado or care for their dignity, everyone scrambled onto the creaking wagon and they set off, the carter's threatened vengeance fading in the distance behind them.

Part Three

The Other Country

» Twenty «

It was Malkin who first noticed the strangeness of the sky. The others were too preoccupied: Gallimaufry trying to persuade the carter's stubborn, nervous horse that he was its new lord and master; Tabor and Pennyroyal, eyes tight shut, gripping each other, wincing as the bone-hard jolts of the cart demonstrated all too plainly what the horse thought of Gallimaufry. Malkin had had her eyes shut too, but a particularly nasty jolt had made them fly wide open, and she turned around in her seat, wondering if they'd actually hit something. She saw, on the horizon behind them, a cloud about the size of a fist, the color of a small, livid bruise. As she watched, the cloud grew rapidly bigger, and she thought she could hear a faint drumming sound within it, like the hooves of a distant horse. Struck by a sudden fear, she surveyed the sky before them—and saw, in the far distance but growing closer, another bruise-colored cloud. If those two clouds joined up, she thought, there would be the grandmama of all storms! The clouds did not look like the familiarly unpredictable workings of nature; there was something strange and terrifying about them. She scrambled to Gallimaufry's side.

"Gallimaufry! Gallimaufry!" she called. "We must find shelter, and quickly!"

Unfortunately her intervention had the effect of making the carter's horse even more convinced of the wisdom and kindness of his former master, and he swerved and bucked, making a desperate attempt to escape. Gallimaufry lost control of the reins altogether, and the cart careered at a fantastic pace down the road, over massive ruts and holes seemingly the size of cathedrals. Meanwhile the sky darkened steadily, the bruise-colored clouds growing even more purple and green around the edges, getting closer and closer. Malkin could no longer hear the drumming, however, as the runaway cart's sturdy wheels were making such an unhallowed noise on the fortunately empty road.

The cart came to an intersection of three roads. Gallimaufry tried one last time to grab the reins, and the horse, feeling this, gave a desperate bellow of rebellion and then galloped headfirst down the middle road. This was not at all the one Gallimaufry would have chosen; indeed, it soon became a deep-rutted track, leading into the entrance of a wood. At that moment there was a massive clap of thunder, and the horse redoubled his desperate pace. Bushes and branches whipped at their faces. With a great noise of splintering and cracking, the cart hit a tree and overturned, spilling its terrified cargo into a tangle of hazel bushes. The horse, freed from the wreckage behind him, did not stop to look at it; he kept going for dear life, and the sound of his fleeing hooves grew steadily fainter and fainter down the track.

For a moment all was silence, the secretive, rustling silence of the wood. No storm here, no rain, no thunder. The four figures lay stunned; first Malkin, then Gallimaufry, then Tabor and Pennyroyal slowly and painfully got to their feet.

"What did you . . ." began Gallimaufry in a justifiably irritated tone, glaring at Malkin. But she put a finger to her lips.

"Listen," she said. Maybe it was the knock on the head, but there was an odd excitement, almost a joy, fizzing in her veins. They listened—and heard the sweet, silver melody of a song they knew well, played on a reed.

Hey ho! To the greenwood now let us go!
Sing heave and ho! And there we will find
both buck and doe; sing heave and ho!

"Why," said Gallimaufry for them all, eyes round, "that was the song I was playing when we first met." He began to sing it softly, as the sound of its melody came nearer and nearer.

The hart and the hind and the pretty little roe.
Sing heave and ho! Hey ho!

The others stood there in a strange, sweet delight. In the wood the light was golden-green and fresh, the trees—oak, ash, aspen, hazel, beech—crisscrossed the air with the soaring tracery of their limbs; the menacing sky was almost forgotten. Yet underneath the silver thread of music, Malkin could still hear a distant, thumping drumming that made her pulse race with unease.

All at once Pug stood before them, his lips on the reed and his eyes dancing green, his rags green too, in the wood-light. He did not speak, but motioned them to him, playing all the while. As he played, the hazel bushes around them wavered and dissolved and they stood in a place they had never seen before, yet which was somehow familiar.

They were in a soaring-ceilinged hall filled with dissolving verticals of golden-green light pouring in through crisscross windows, like an airy cathedral. It was full of people, all looking at them. Sweet music played, music that filled them with a longing to hear more. Malkin glanced at her companions. They were staring, their eyes full of enchantment, their mouths open in soundless wonder. She wished she could be like them, but the drumming she had heard in the cloud still pounded insistently in her pulse. She looked at the hall and saw its beauty, but saw too the shadows gathering in the corners, the leers on some of the faces watching them, the heavy wood-smell of decaying matter that snaked in from somewhere, and all at once she felt giddy with fear.

Then Pug touched her elbow gently, and grinned. "Such a long, solemn face!" he said. "Open your heart, and you have nothing to fear. Look well on these things, for they are all things that you know. See deeply, and there is nothing to be afraid of."

So saying, he propelled her by the elbow, motioning to the other three to follow, and the little procession made its way to the front of the hall. There Pug stopped, made a deep but somehow mocking bow, and said, "Your Majesties, here they are."

He was addressing a man and a woman who were of medium height and of a commanding appearance. They were dressed in greens and golds and russets, like autumn trees—had autumn trees worn silks and velvets. The man had long curly hair the color of rich, dark earth, and eyes of a startling summer blue; the woman, straight, flowing hair the color of a clear silver forest stream, and eyes of a golden amber as glowing as the fires of the Earth. Their lips curved in a kind of smile; then the Queen said, in a rather bored tone: "Good. It is time to call an end to this. I am tired of it all."

"I would remind you, my love," said the King impatiently, as if this were an old argument, "that this was your own idea."

The Queen just shrugged. "I did not ask you to claim it, Oberon, my sweet," she observed coldly. Then she turned to Pug. "You have done well. But they are dirty; they smell; they look like scarecrows. Get them cleaned up and bring them back."

She had scarcely looked at them, beyond a first disdainful glance, but Tabor, Pennyroyal, and Gallimaufry gazed at her in astonished delight, as if every word emerging from her thin lips were a pearl or a diamond. Malkin, however, looked at the man and the woman with a hollow feeling of familiarity, and to comfort herself grasped at the gold heart that still hung at her throat under her ragged clothes. Instantly she felt herself to be clothed in the feather dress, the cap of moss on her head, the green grass shoes on her feet. The woman looked at her, her eyes locked on Malkin's, and silence fell on the hall.

"But *this one*," said the Queen, "she is to stay." An odd expression had come into her fine eyes. Malkin would almost have called it uncertainty.

Pug bowed again and beckoned to the others to follow him. And it was then that the rustling silence of the hall, so like the rustling silence of the wood, became almost more than Malkin could bear.

"Why are we here?" she shouted. "I did not ask to come here. We are looking for our friend Tattercoats, and we must keep seeking her."

"Is that all?" said the Queen. She smiled, and clicked a finger. "Bring them." And shadows at the edges of the hall moved shivering away, flowing toward the doors.

Malkin waited, trying to still her fluttering heart, meeting the Queen's gaze with an uneasy defiance.

The King gazed at them both in some amusement, his glance flicking from the Queen to Malkin and back again. Finally he laughed, throwing back his head as if he were greatly amused. "My dear Titania, it seems that you are at a loss for once!" Turning to Malkin, he said: "This I have waited a long time to see: my Titania made uneasy! The queen of my heart embarrassed by her own willful pride! Remember, my heart, the donkey's head, and be careful!"

He could have been quacking like a duck, for all Malkin could understand what he was saying. But she could see that Titania was very annoyed, for she turned an angry shoulder on him and focused fully on Malkin.

"Tell me," she said in her golden-honey voice, "do you truly not recognize us? I held you in my arms long ago. Do you not remember that?"

Malkin stared at her, her heart fluttering again; but before she could reply, the door at the end of the hall opened, and through it stepped two figures in the midst of a guard of silent soldiers: a man, tall, broad, dressed all in black, his cloak flying around him like a raven's wing, his face hidden under a silk domino mask, but the silver bristles of what had once been a beard clearly visible on his chin; and a girl, small, plump as a robin, with long red hair flaming on her shoulders. Tattercoats—and the Baron!

» Twenty-one «

Malkin could not help but cry out. At the sound the hall filled with whisperings and murmurings, and Titania called out imperiously, "Silence!"

Oberon smiled. "You will always have your own way," he murmured happily. But he was ignored by the Queen, who beckoned Tattercoats and the Baron to come closer.

"Is this what you were looking for?" she said to Malkin.

"Who, not what," said Malkin defiantly. She looked at her friend. Tattercoats was dressed, like the others in the court, in clothes of forest splendor, and her eyes were at once blank and merry.

"Tattercoats," said the Queen, "here is your friend, who has been looking for you." Her voice was sharp and dry now. "Are you not happy to see her?"

Tattercoats smiled blissfully but did not speak. She turned her laughing, empty eyes on Malkin and nodded brightly.

Malkin's eyes filled with tears. She took a step toward Tattercoats. "Oh, Tattercoats, we have looked for you everywhere," she said. "Are you . . . can you speak to me? Tell me you are well, that all is well with you?" Tattercoats still gazed at her with that bright, happy, empty look. Malkin's throat felt thick with the pain of it. "Don't you know me, Tattercoats?" she whispered. She put out her hand toward the other girl, but before she could touch her, the man with her, the wicked Baron, stepped forward and took her arm, propelling her back behind him. His eyes through the mask were steady and fiery, but he did not speak at all. Malkin felt unsteady on her feet as she thought of what might be planned for his granddaughter, here in this beautiful, menacing place. And where was Oscuro? Was all this his doing?

Titania snapped, "Take them away!"

"But I thought," said Malkin, and the words came from deep inside her, where memory was returning, overwhelming her. "I thought Pug said Tattercoats was under the protection of the Other Country. This is the Other Country, isn't it? The fairy country. And you are its Queen and King. Why does she look as if she is a prisoner here? As if she is not herself anymore? Why doesn't she speak to me?"

Titania was still. Malkin heard Oberon's snicker, but the Queen ignored it. "She is under our protection," said the Queen at last. "Don't play games with me. She is safe, as are all your foolish friends. You know the rules. There is no way around them for us."

Malkin thought she saw the Baron's eyes flicker beneath the mask. She said: "Although you speak to me as if I should know the rules you mention, Lady, I know nothing of them. Tattercoats has done no harm—has never done any harm. Is this contemptuous treatment your *protection*? If you are truly Queen of the Other Country, my Lady, why do you allow this . . . this raven to take her? He only wishes her ill. He has always wished her ill, or ignored her, which can be worse. If I had known that's what Pug meant by protection, I would have broken his reed and made feather pillows out of his geese!" Full of angry sorrow, she stood her ground and glared at Titania.

"Oh good, good!" said Oberon, coming toward her, applauding ironically. "Now, Titania," he observed, "you must agree you are truly worsted. There is no help for it but to tell the girl the truth." He peered at Malkin. "You please me. You are not afraid, or glamour-struck. You have a strong spirit, as I had hoped!" At his words the hall erupted in cheers and whistles and clappings, and Malkin saw that the Baron's eyes were darting wildly around, and Tattercoats's were beginning to focus, slowly.

Titania shrugged ferociously. She snapped her fingers, and the guard of soldiers reformed around the girl and her grandfather. "Take them away. Bring them back later, when this one shows more respect and understanding." Then, as Malkin helplessly watched Tattercoats go, escorted by the Baron, the Queen turned to Oberon. "You are too easily satisfied, Oberon. I will not stand by and be insulted by this . . . this girl, who does not even understand the gratitude of the belly. Look at how much we have given her and her fine friends! And still she denies us and thwarts us!"

It was Oberon's turn to shrug. "You made your bed; you must lie in it," he observed. "You always want to be subtle and proceed in riddles. You should have let the girl know the truth from the beginning, as I suggested. But no, it must be your way, your idea, from beginning to end."

He looked at Titania haughtily, and Malkin could see the Queen's lips puckering for another volley in their private war; Malkin felt heartily sick of it all. She burst out: "Your Majesties, you may know what you are talking about, but I do not. I am tired of riddles and silences and illusions. I want to know why we are here and what you plan to do with us! I don't know you, no matter what you say. Nor do I wish to. I am not sure I . . . I would wish to, anyway," she went on, defiantly. "All I know is that my friend Tattercoats is being held prisoner here, and that my friend Pug, whom I thought true, is treacherous. Please . . ." and her eyes filled with tears. "Please, kind Sir, kind Lady, if you are indeed masters of this place, take pity on us. We have done nothing wrong to any of you."

There was a silence. Titania looked at Malkin, biting her lip a little, as if she were thinking; but Oberon, after a moment, said, "Girl . . ."

"Malkin," she corrected. She tried to sound firm, but her voice trembled a little.

"Malkin then," said Oberon, and his smile was oddly kind. "Malkin, I will tell you a story." There was a movement from Titania, but he quelled it with a wave of his hand. Gazing at him, Malkin's sore heart felt a little easier. It wasn't that she trusted him, exactly—there was too much caprice about him and his kingdom to make trust a wholly binding thing in this place—but she knew suddenly that neither he nor Titania meant any of them any harm. It was simply that you could not understand things here with logic, reason, or daylight eyes; like Pug's spells, this was a place of dream-knowledge. The People of Peace, the fairies, she remembered, were never evil, though they were not innocent either. Perhaps, in a strange way, they were to be pitied, even. It was a new thought, but oddly, comforting.

"Once there was a handsome young man," the King began, still smiling. "He was engaged to a pretty young woman, the only child of her widowed father, who lived in a castle by the edge of a wood. One day, after visiting his lady love, the young man was riding home through the wood when his horse tripped over a root and the man fell heavily on his head. When he awoke he found himself in a beautiful country he had never seen before. The loveliest maiden he had ever seen was looking at him with a gentle smile. She did not speak. She held out her arms, and the young man fell into them and forgot everything but that embrace. Then she took him by the hand, and they loved each other for a long time. The young woman was the beloved foster daughter of the Queen of that place, who was very pleased that her child had found such happiness. But little by little the young man's memories of his earlier life returned, and he began to pine for his other country. He pined and pined—so much that the maiden grew sad, then angry. She sent him away, far from her, back to that other place he loved so much, and that other girl. But the maiden herself was with child. She had not told the young man, for she believed he must choose freely and not be tied by silken webs. The child was born, but the young woman grew paler and thinner and sadder, and the Queen, her foster mother, could do nothing to help her. The Queen would have caused great havoc to fall on the lover and his family, but her daughter refused and made her give a binding promise that she would always look after the child, and its father, and anyone who was connected with him, for as long as all of them would live. The Queen was angry, but she could not refuse her foster daughter anything. When the young woman slipped away into death one morning, the Queen was inconsolable. She was left with the baby, who was a scrawny child with her father's eyes, and who cried constantly, never-endingly, as if she knew of the tragedy of her mother. One day, at her wits' end, the Queen cried out, '*Oh, turn into a raven and fly away to the country of the*

121

mortals where you belong, and do not bother me any longer!' And at that moment the child gave a piercing cry, turned into a raven, and flew out of the window, never to be seen again. Then the Queen ran to the window and made a spell, calling out after the winged child: *'When you reach your father's country, you will be a baby again, and grow, though your life will not be easy. You will always be under my eye, accompanied. And one day you wll return here, by difficult paths, and you will make your choice.'''* Oberon's voice faded away, and he was silent. Titania's eyes were on Malkin, and Malkin knew there was a question in her gaze—an uncertain, doubting thing strange to see in her fine, determined eyes. Pug had come back into the hall too, and he was standing by Malkin. All at once he reached out, and gently, briefly clasped her hand. The tears started in her eyes, for she knew by that touch that Pug was still her true friend, and that his reason for bringing her here was nothing like treachery at all, no matter what her rash words had been earlier. Oberon's story had stirred something deep, deep in her soul that was bubbling up to the surface, and she knew that when it did she would understand everything that had happened, would make sense of it all, and that she would never be the same again.

She opened her mouth to speak—but at that very moment, there was a tremendous crash, a thunder of hooves, and something came flying in through the crisscross windows of the hall, sending shattered shards of glass everywhere—glass that dissolved as soon as it touched the ground. In the midst of the vanishing fragments, eyes shut, hat askew, locks disordered, was Oscuro, clutching in one hand what appeared to be a wand of hazel wood.

"My horse," he moaned, his eyes still shut. "My horse—bloody English horses, as bad-tempered and contrary as the humans." He opened one eye, shut it again very quickly, and moaned again. "No, oh, my head hurts, it hurts, I am dead, maybe . . ."

Oberon had crossed over to where Oscuro lay. His handsome, sharp face was alight with a peculiar joy. "I have my own surprises, Titania," he said.

» Twenty-two «

Titania was at their side in a moment. "How dare you!" she stormed. Malkin saw that the Queen's face had an odd livid tinge to it, a color rather like that of the cloud that had bruised the sky. But Oberon, crossing his arms, said, "My love, it seems to me that we have meddled enough in the affairs of these people, and that it is time to set it all right, for all of them. Your way is not the only way, Titania, my love."

Titania glowered at him. She said, "But what is the purpose of bringing this . . . this sorry sight here?"

"I am begging your pardon," said Oscuro, smiling in a rather humble fashion. He *did* look a rather sorry sight, his beautiful clothes dusty and torn, his winged cloak hanging crooked, his hair fallen out of its careful curls, the dark brown roots clearly showing in what was now revealed to be *dyed* blond hair. "I am sorry, but I am dizzy; I am ill; I am imagining things. I, who have never dreamed, am now in a dream! This cannot be really happening—magic is only the domain of the conjuror, and not real!" He shook his head like a dog, then looked up hopefully, as if expecting that now his head would be clear and the world obediently back in its controllable place. It was this that made Malkin realize that the Italian magician was just as bewildered by what had happened as she was herself, and in that case he surely could not be the instrument of Tattercoats's kidnapping and enthrallment in this perilous realm, despite what she had overheard in the Baron's castle before they had run away. The Baron had spoken of "the People of Peace," and how his daughter was a prisoner there and he would need to pay a human tithe before she could be freed. She had thought then that the "human tithe" was to be Tattercoats herself! Did that mean the Baron had acted on his own behalf? But how could he? And why was Oscuro here? It didn't make sense.

She sighed. No one here would give her a straight answer, that was clear. She shook her head impatiently, and the movement caught Oscuro's eye. He looked like he had been whacked in the face by a large, wet fish: sweet revenge indeed. She saw his lips begin to form a sentence: *"What are you doing . . ."* but Oberon spoke before Oscuro could finish.

"This . . . sorry sight, as you so wisely call him, Titania, was a danger not only to others but to himself. He has some skills of his own, some small understanding of glamour. In fact, he has been using our name in vain, Titania—telling the foolish Baron we are after a human tithe in the form of his granddaughter, as if we were demons, and not fairies. He's been saying that he knows how our realm works, and that he has influence here." He smiled at Titania's gathering frown. "Yes, my love, terrible, is it not? It is possible that he has indeed had dealings in the past with some of the fairy kind, perhaps in his own country, and thinks he can trade on it for himself. It could be, too, that he thinks we do not exist, and that he is safe making up his lies. Whatever it may be, we could not leave him to his foolish meddlings; you know that. This was the only way to keep him out of harm's way."

"And now this cheeky quack, this rude charlatan, this disrespectful crook, this false mystifier clutters my hall!" said Titania fiercely, punctuating her words with a well-aimed kick at Oscuro. "Get up."

Oscuro scrambled to his feet. "My Lady," he said ingratiatingly, "if I have offended in some way, may I be allowed to make amends? I know a very little, a very little of the ways of the fairy kingdoms and I . . ."

"Be quiet," ordered Titania. *"There is no king in power here. I am in charge."* Her eyes narrowed as she caught sight of the hazel wand he still clutched. "What is that?"

"If it please Your Majesty," stammered Oscuro, "it is my magic wand."

"Give me that at once." Titania held out an imperious hand. Oscuro looked at Oberon, at Malkin, at the assembled company, but there was no help to be had in any of these faces. He handed the hazel wand to the Queen, who examined it carefully, and then, in a quick movement, broke it in two and threw the pieces behind her. "That will teach you to use toys you don't even understand!" Titania said. "The powers of hazel are not for the likes of you. And so you should know if you have truly been in the fairy realms. Magic wands indeed!"

Oberon smiled at her. "Truly said, my love." He turned languidly to Oscuro. "Titania hates them, you know. She dislikes anything like that: words of power, magic wands, witchy murmurings, magic smoke . . . foolish mortal attempts to control the Other Country. You are fortunate, my friend, that the Queen of the Otherland has not already turned you into a frog or a toad or a worm or given you a hump. But it's not too late yet, is it, Titania, my sweet?"

"Certainly it is not," said Titania. She smiled, and her smile was somehow more frightening than her rage.

Oscuro babbled, "I'm sorry . . . Ma'am . . . Your Majesty . . . my Lady . . . truly, I did not mean to cause offense. The . . . the wand was given to me by an old man at the crossroads. He told me that thus could I . . . I . . . obtain what I wanted. But, truly, I did not know what to do with it!"

"Oberon!" said Titania sharply. "Was that your doing?"

Oberon waved a careless hand. "Had to persuade him in somehow, you know." He smiled unconcernedly at Titania's glare.

"I'm no magician, really I'm not," went on Oscuro. "I'm a charlatan really—a quack. It's so easy in England, because I'm Italian, and they think we are all adept at the black arts, and so, you see, I need to earn my living, we all do, Ma'am. I'm a false mystifier, maybe, Ma'am, but I'm a good one, entertaining, you know, and good at what I do. Ask Malkin, here . . ." he went on eagerly, turning to the young woman. "Isn't that so, Lady?"

Malkin nodded dumbly, but Titania snorted. "False magic! Conjuring! So what? Any fool can do that."

Her tone would have made even the bravest heart quail, but whatever faults Oscuro had, he was not timid. He drew himself up. "Ma'am, I pride myself on my skill. People do get what they are looking for, with me, even though it may not be real magic, like here . . ."

Malkin stared at him, nonplussed.

He caught her gaze and flushed. It made him look all at once much younger, more uncertain, and considerably more appealing. He drew himself up defiantly. "Yes, I'm a charlatan, Ma'am. A good one. I make my own publicity. Everyone thinks I'm so bad and wicked, a magician, a poisoner, a frightener. It's quite useful. But I have never hurt anyone really. I just give them what they want. Most of them can't stand truth or honesty. Glamour, is it? Mystery? I know a hundred tricks, and can persuade anyone of my fairy powers and other such foolishness . . ."

Too late he realized what he had said. Titania's eyes flashed. She waved a hand in the air. "You lack respect. And you still lie. So be a drone. Fill the air with your buzzing importance."

"That was rather splendidly done, my love," said Oberon admiringly, as a rather bedraggled bumblebee made its lumbering flight through the hall. As it passed Malkin, she was startled to see that the insect's face still had Oscuro's violet eyes, eyes that fixed on her in an expression of such hopelessness that her stomach lurched. It was the last thing she would ever have expected, but at that moment Malkin pitied Oscuro with all her heart. It appeared she had been mistaken about him all along.

Titania saw Malkin's expression. She shrugged. "He is no loss, that mortal. He would have put you in great danger, with no qualms, for his own advantage. Offered you an alliance, did he?" She smiled without amusement at Malkin's startled face. "He would have betrayed you at the first opportunity. Mortals are like that—two-faced, untrustworthy, concerned with worthless things like war and power and money. And those like him are even more dangerous, for they think they know more than most." She snapped her fingers again and turned to Pug, standing silently behind her. "Here," she said, handing him the gilded, glass-walled little cage that had appeared in her hand. "Put that sorry creature in there, and give him to Malkin."

Pug shrugged. He caught Malkin's eye, but went obediently in search of the bumblebee that was now hitting bewilderedly at the walls of the hall. He came back with the insect safely imprisoned in the glass cage.

"There," said Titania triumphantly, "my gift to you. He can do no more harm this way." She looked briefly at the panicked drone in the cage, and smiled. "Not so clever now, my friend, are you?" She held out the cage to Malkin, who took it reluctantly.

Inside the glass the drone was still butting at the walls, trying in vain to get out. Titania watched, still with that satisfied smile, a smile that made Malkin feel queasy. It is not because Oscuro is dangerous that Titania has done this to him, Malkin thought. It is because he *lacked in respect* to her. Aloud, she said stiffly: "I do not know why I should have this. I am not his keeper."

"True. It may be easier simply to crush the sorry thing," said Oberon, softly.

"NO!" said Malkin, taking a step backward and clutching the cage.

Oberon smiled, and Titania frowned. But before she could speak, Pug said hastily, "Your Majesties, the three other mortals with Malkin wish to give their gifts to you."

"Gifts!" said Titania. "It is strange and unusual that mortals should be so polite. Bring them here then. Let us see these . . . gifts."

"Yes, Your Majesty," said Pug. His gaze was fixed on Malkin's, as if he were trying to tell her something. Then she saw his lips framing the words: "Wait. Wait and see."

Wait and see, she thought furiously. We are prisoners here, all of us, prisoners. Oscuro's power had been shown to be an empty thing, despite all his mysteries and boasting, but Tattercoats was still the prey of the old raven, the Baron. And here, who knew what might happen? Once again she thought of that human tithe, and shivered as she remembered the stories the country folk told of the Otherland, of the People of Peace, of Titania's people. . . . Oberon had said they did not take human tithes, that they were not demons, but what exactly did they want? What would they do to Tattercoats? What would Titania want with her? An unwelcome thought entered Malkin's mind. She herself was the only one to whom the King and Queen had spoken with any semblance of civility. Why was this so? And what was the meaning of Oberon's story? Who was the lover? Who the mother? Who the child? Surely the child must be Tattercoats; the Queen, Titania herself . . . But then she knew for sure that Margaret, the old Baron's daughter, had been Tattercoats's mother. And she had been truly human, not fairy at all. Yet Oberon's tale could also explain Oscuro's strange story, the one about Tattercoats's royal provenance. It had not been *English* royal ancestry at all, but from the Otherworld! Oscuro had gotten it all wrong, had gotten hold of quite the bluntest end of the stick. Poor Oscuro, she thought, and strangely did not enjoy the thought of his undoing.

Oberon's attitude could also easily be explained. Perhaps he had married Titania only after the raven child had flown away. He must be consort only. This was a queendom, like England, and it was Titania who held the power. That explained Oberon's peculiarly amused, rather sly attitude. He was perhaps not used to having one over his royal wife, and it amused him to see her dance on the end of her own harpoon.

But Pug . . . Pug, her friend. It was strange and almost fearful to know he was from such a place. It was fearful to think that he must have known Oscuro's true nature, and yet had hurried them away from the castle. And all for what? So that Tattercoats could be not only in the power of the Baron but of this strange and ambiguous realm? Surely not! Yet the question still troubled her, despite her feeling that Pug was still very much her friend; but was he Tattercoats's friend too?

Meanwhile Titania and Oberon were conferring in soft voices at some distance, heads close together. The hall was still full of that beautiful light, though shadows were lengthening in all its corners. Around the King and Queen flowed the rustling, ru-tilant crowds of their people, and Malkin looked at them prop-erly for the first time. There were many who looked just like ordinary—well, all right, *extraordinary*—mortals, like Titania and Oberon, but others were creatures of dream: dwarves with red caps and red eyes; tiny wispy creatures that at first glance Malkin had taken to be dragonflies but now appeared to have a vague-ly human shape; tall figures with long green hair and long, flaking, twiglike arms; small, jolly-looking people with long pointed ears; and, in the furthest shadows, things out of nightmare rather than dream. Malkin caught a glimpse of green teeth, eyes of fire, and lank drowned hair before turning away quickly again. Around all these creatures' feet roamed silent dogs: some pure white with red ears and eyes, others dark as the night, but all restless, searching, sniffing.

The odd thing was that this strange place felt like a dream version, a distorted mirror image, of Elizabeth's court. There too were the splendors and beauties and fun of the dazzling English court, but also dangerous, frightening things hiding not in the corners of the hall but in the recesses of human hearts. Shadow, dream, mirror: truly, she thought, Titania and Oberon ruled over a perilous realm! It was then that she noticed something that at first meant very little: although the Otherland courtiers were richly dressed, not one of them wore a sword or rapier or even dagger, where Elizabeth's courtiers would have displayed beauti-fully worked weapons of Toledo steel and gleaming iron, coldly shining. The People of Peace *indeed,* she smiled to herself. There must be no sudden quarrels or quick-tempered pride here! But then, there was no need to; what weapons were of any use against the powerful fairy magic?

She looked at the insect inside its glass cage. It was huddled in a crumpled heap, unmoving. Malkin thought of what it must be like to be suddenly spirited into such a shape. She shivered, and unconsciously stroked at the glass wall, making the drone feebly wave one of its legs and buzz softly. Malkin's heart turned over, for though the insect who was Oscuro could not speak, nevertheless it seemed to her as if she could make out words in the pitiful buzzing. "Forgive me," it seemed to say to her. "Forgive me, Malkin—I did not know what I was doing."

Malkin could not speak at first, but stroked the glass, very gently. There was a great lump in her throat. How could she think of Oscuro as her enemy anymore, when he was so helpless? It would be wicked indeed to deny him comfort, even if she could do little. So, carefully, she brought the glass up close to her, as if she were examining it, and managed to whisper, "I promise you this, Oscuro: If we get out of here, I will do everything I can to help you regain your normal shape." Quite how she would do that, she had no idea at all. But perhaps something would come to her later.

At that moment, Pug came back with Pennyroyal, Gallimaufry, and Tabor, and Malkin quickly lowered her arm. Titania and Oberon had not seen, though; they had been too busy conferring together. Now everyone was quiet and still as the three approached. Malkin's friends looked scrubbed to within an inch of their skins, and their borrowed fairy finery, obviously made for more delicate frames, hung rather awkwardly on them. But they seemed cheerful enough..

"Malkin!" whispered Pennyroyal when they had all four reached her. "Isn't this a wonderful place!"

"Yes," nodded Tabor, "truly wonderful."

"Full of *wonder*, am I," said Gallimaufry, his eyes wide and guileless. "I'd always dreamt of going to fairyland, to the land of the Sidhe, as we call it at home in Ireland! They truly appreciate good poetry and music, you know, Malkin; unlike those philistines out in the mortal world who can't tell a fashionable donkey-versifier from a true poet!"

Malkin shrugged despondently. "Wonder, wonder, wonder," she said. She sighed, and said, more to Pug than to the others, who had not even noticed the glass cage and were looking around them in delight: "But I am not sure what will happen. I don't know why we are here."

"*Still* you do not remember?" said Pug, and a curious sadness flashed into his green eyes.

"Mortal time effaces the memory," said Oberon, who was now standing by them. "I have noticed that. Mortals are creatures of so little time."

He and Pug looked at each other, and in their gaze Malkin read the eternal, sad patience of the immortal. It wrung her heart, suddenly, so that she cried: "There is something I do see, but it is as in a pond, muddily; there is no mirror-clearness in my mind. Oh, Sire," turning to Oberon, "if you would but enlighten me, so that we could all know what it is you want!"

Oberon shook his head. "I cannot tell you; not yet, Malkin. The time has not yet come. Everything must come at the appointed time or the spell will never be wholly lifted."

But Malkin hardly heard him. For she had suddenly remembered just what the People of Peace, the dwellers of the Otherland, were supposed to be afraid of. Iron. Cold iron. Iron forged by mortals and shaped into things. But why? How would this sudden memory help? And why did the thought leave her feeling so sad?

» Twenty-three «

"Ambergold," said Pennyroyal to Titania, curtsying nervously. "Love-lies-bleeding-no-more, Your Majesties . . ." In her hands the little bottles gleamed, little jewels of sunrise and dewdrop. The court was silent, everyone holding their breath, as Titania examined the bottles, unstoppered them, sniffed, and smiled. There was a noticeable exhalation of collective breath. . . .

"Pretty," she remarked. "Not as fine as our work, but not bad, for mortals." She beckoned to two wispy little creatures behind her. "Observe, Cobweb, Mustardseed. You may take these and put them in our perfumery. What say you, Oberon? Perhaps a new flower, an original plant?"

"A good idea," said Oberon smoothly.

Cobweb and Mustardseed took the bottles, their pointed little faces aglow. Titania smiled again. "Not bad," she repeated. She looked at Pennyroyal. "One gift deserves another." She reached out and gently touched Pennyroyal's left hand. "In this be perfect measure. A fortune be in your hands."

"Oh, th-thank you," stammered Pennyroyal.

Oberon said: "Really, my love, you should explain more. It would save an awful lot of trouble later." He turned to Pennyroyal. "When you return to your own country, you will find that all will flock to you for perfumes and tonics. You will become famous, with your own shop that will become renowned, even to the court itself."

"Ohh . . ." breathed Pennyroyal. She gazed at Titania. "Your Majesty, you are so kind . . ."

Malkin saw that tears had sprung up in Pennyroyal's eyes. But Titania had already turned away, to Gallimaufry, who stood dazzled behind Pennyroyal.

"Yes?" she said in her peremptory way, and despite herself, the Queen's tone made Malkin smile inwardly.

Gallimaufry said to Titania, "Oh, my Lady, I do not have much to give except for my poor little songs . . ."

"I hope they're not too poor," answered Titania sharply. "For if there's anything we dislike, it's an offkey voice and slack verse. But we reward good poetry and music."

Gallimaufry colored, and swallowed, and Malkin, remembering his earlier words, would have smiled at the contrast in his earlier boastfulness and his present uncertainty. But it really was not that funny, not here. "Your Majesty," he began, very nervously. "I . . ." But he stopped abruptly, for at that moment there was a rustle at the end of the hall, and Tattercoats, followed by the Baron, came in.

Gallimaufry made a pleased movement toward her, holding out his hand in greeting; but Tattercoats gazed at her love blankly and cheerfully, as if he were a pleasant stranger, and passed straight past him to stand near Titania. Gallimaufry stopped, blinked, bent his head, and began to sing the song he had fashioned in London:

Is it a lord I am? Or just a dream?
Do I sleep? If that I seem
Not to know, and ask of you
To tell the truth, and tell it true,
Why then, I speak, I know, I see;
I hear a pleasant melody.
Away, away shake off my sleep,
And hold to what I keep:
My foolish fancies are no more,
For I live now, who did but dream before . . .

There was a yearning in his voice, a sadness that had not been there before, and somehow it filled the little song with a depth of emotion that seemed to resonate through the whole hall. Malkin saw a puzzled look in Tattercoats's eyes, slowly changing, changing, becoming clearer, memory beginning to return. She could feel tears start in her own eyes; Gallimaufry's voice had never seemed so sweet, and the pangs of love never more affecting.

There was silence when he finished, then applause from the court and an excited whispering that went on and on. Oberon looked at Titania, and she nodded.

"Always be welcome in the Other Country," she said decisively. "Soar like a bird, and bring the tears to a stone. That will be your fortune; greater still than that of a king."

"She means," Oberon said patiently, "that you will be known as a fashioner of wonderful songs, that you will become not only rich and famous but immortal too through your songs."

Now, from being sad, the mercurial Gallimaufry burst into tears of joy, and Tattercoats came to his side then, murmuring and troubled. She patted his hand, and he clasped hers fervently. It was clear that wonder and happiness were returning to his hopeful, merry heart. If only, Malkin thought, if only I could feel that way.

Titania smiled. "A pretty sight indeed, young love," she murmured. "Now you, fine Sir . . ." turning to Tabor.

Tabor was standing before Titania with his eyes goggling, his mouth opening and closing. He seemed incapable of doing anything at all. Titania frowned.

"Your gift, Sir? Where is your gift? Did they not teach you well in your country? When you are before a queen, Sir, you do not stare like a googly fish, Sir!" Her hand started to rise, but Oberon caught it gently and held it.

"The poor man is overcome by your wonders, my love," he said softly.

There was a rustle and a whisper in the hall, an expectant, almost gloating sound as all waited for Tabor to speak. At Malkin's wrist the glass cage jiggled: the drone was buzzing loudly inside his prison. For a moment Malkin looked at the insect. Oscuro's eyes, magnified by the glass, stared back at her, mutely pleading. Iron. Cold iron. She must use cold iron and free them all from Titania's perilous realm, which though it might not be evil, was perilous indeed. She knew now that danger did not always come in darkness and shadows; it could be clothed in golden-green light, shine in the imperious gaze of one so powerful who cared little for ordinary human warmth. But what to use? She had taken a knife with her from Fisher Forest, but she had long ago lost it, and in any case, she had the feather dress on now. She had no iron thing with her at all. She put a nervous hand to her throat, and as her fingers brushed the warm gold of her locket, she heard Pug's whisper. "Not all iron is in the hand. Look in your heart, my dear. Look in your heart." His voice was infinitely sad, and it made her want to weep.

She jerked her attention back to the scene before her. Titania was looking at Tabor expressionlessly. Yet Malkin could feel, humming in her like a song, the angry magic beginning to gather around Tabor's hapless head. There was no telling what Titania would do. She had her own reasons for everything, for she was a queen of great power and majesty, and they were merely simple humans, pawns in her game of caprice.

Malkin took a step forward. "Tabor," she said urgently. "Tabor, you must speak."

He turned his head toward her helplessly, dazzled like Gallimaufry but less blessed.

"Tabor," she said again. "Remember, Tabor. Remember your favorite time, your heart's song. Give it to the gracious Queen."

Pug was standing still with his pointed ears somehow sad and drooping, and his reed halfway to his mouth. Then suddenly Tabor began, at first haltingly, as if repeating words he could barely hear, but getting louder and more confident as he went on. "I will give you the song of King Henri . . . I will give you the song of my youth, and the clashing of steel, and the lifting of cups, and the look in a lady's eye!"

He began to drum gently, and to sing, in a voice that started off soft and tentative but soon became firmer, louder, stronger. And as he drummed, Pug, too, began to play on his reed, so that the melody skipped and hopped pleasantly and cheerfully, making them all tap their feet:

Long live King Henri!
Long live our joyous King!
Long live his memory
In all of these three things:
Clash of steel, and valor, and skill in the art of love!:

He sang it once, twice, three times. The third time was not in English but in French. If there had been a rustling and a whispering before, there was now silence, total silence. And then an unexpected thing happened. Another voice took up the song, first soft, then getting louder, louder. Spinning around, Malkin saw that the Baron—the *Baron!*—was singing lustily, his head thrown back.

At last the song ended. The Baron spoke. "Thank the stars," he said, and his voice was not that of the Lord of Fisher Forest. "Thank the moon," he said, as he took off the mask that had covered his face and revealed features that were not that of the Baron of Fisher Forest. "Thank the heavens," he said, and smiled uncertainly. "I can speak at long last." Malkin stared. She had never seen this man before. She was looking at a perfect stranger.

Tattercoats detached herself from Gallimaufry and ran toward him. "Father," she cried. "So it is really you! I *knew* you'd be back to get me. I knew!" She threw herself into his arms.

"Dear girl," said Will de Montacour, looking rather shamefaced. He stroked her hair. "I . . ." Then he looked at Titania, and sketched a bow. "I am sorry," he said in a low voice. "It is against all the rules. I know I am not allowed to speak in your realm, as I offended against you previously, but I could not help myself. I have sat with le Roi Henri myself. I have raised cups to him. That song made my own fortune . . . I can't forget . . ." He smiled rather hopelessly, and gabbled: "My Lady, I know your powers. I did truly want to make amends, not only for the past. You understand, my main failing is talking too much. I was too free in my cups that night, a year ago when the Italian magician heard my babbling and brought such danger upon us. And then telling my daughter, my Susanna, who I really was before I brought her here; I know I was not supposed to, but she was so sad, so frightened, my Lady. Now she has spoken too and has broken the protection spell around her. It is my fault, all of this, only mine. Please spare them. Only punish me. In my defense, I kept my word and did not tell him the real truth, only a garbled version of it, though perhaps that was even less wise. I know I deserve the punishment you might see fit to give me, for you have been more than kind with me . . . and my daughters. Yet for the sake of the one we both cared for . . ." His voice dwindled away into silence.

Titania did not shrug. She did not look haughty. Her expression was frozen, almost perfectly blank. She raised one hand.

"No. Stop!" said a voice strong and clear, and for a moment Malkin did not even realize it was hers. "Stop. In the name of iron, Queen Titania, in the name of cold iron, I ask you to retreat." At her wrist the cage jiggled madly as the drone buzzed frantically against the glass.

The court rose up as one body, advancing inexorably toward her. Malkin could see the creatures of dream and nightmare swirling up in a cloud around the frozen figures of the King and Queen of the Otherland. But worse than that sight was the sadness, almost unbearable in its steeliness, cutting through her like a knife.

"Oh, Malkin, what did you think I was going to do? Never would I have harmed you, or yours. I held you in my arms once," came Titania's whispering voice. "Held you in my arms and looked on you. Then I turned you into a raven and you flew away and were gone. You were a granddaughter to me once, long ago. Oh, child of mine, daughter of my dearest friend, would you be faithless too? Faithless, faithless, like that man who is your father; your father, as he is also the father of your friend, your Tattercoats . . ."

Titania's words filled Malkin's ears, her heart, her soul.

"Oh, Malkin, remember, remember, remember. We do not know love quite as you do, we People of Peace, but neither do we know hate. We were punished for rebelling against the rule of heaven, but we are not evil, Malkin. We are loyal and true to our mortal friends, and we know the sadness of the immortal as all our mortal friends disappear so quickly, so swiftly! Don't drive us away, Malkin. Don't put cold iron between us. . . . Don't forget, Malkin . . .'"

The knife of longing had pierced Malkin's heart now, and in its terrible pain, she understood at last who she was. It was she who was the raven child. It was she, not Tattercoats, who had the fairy glamour, the fairy protection. This, the Otherland, was *her* country, and Titania and Oberon, her almost-kin. She was a changeling, a halfling, and she belonged here. But she had cast it all away for her purely human companions. Her eyes swam with tears.

Around her the court was already fading, the hall full of shadows. But Will de Montacour was staring at her, smiling humbly, and Pug was nowhere to be seen. Then she heard Oberon's voice, though she could no longer see him, patiently explaining.

"Yes, my dear, dear Malkin, you are almost one of us. Your mother was a dearly beloved mortal changeling child of my Queen, and when she died for love of your faithless father, Will, my sweet Titania was inconsolable. And when she is sad, she becomes angry, does things she regrets later. She could not touch your faithless father because of her promise. But she turned you into a raven and sent you away, and was sorry, so sorry afterward. Always she watched over you; yes, over you, and over that faithless man's other daughter, for your sake, and because your mother had bound her to do so. She even sent a guardian to watch over you. Yes, the one you know as Pug, who can move between both worlds. She sent also the feather dress, to help you come into your inheritance again. And your friend, the mortal Tattercoats, she was to lead you to us, because we do not walk on easy roads, Malkin, we go by hidden ways. We could not just bid you come to us because then your journey would have achieved nothing. We gave her gifts so that you would be gifted too—the precious gift of the open heart, which knows and sees so much." The voice died away to a whisper, a thin, sad whisper. "Oh, Malkin! Why did you put cold iron on us? It drives us away not because we are afraid of it but because it shows you have no need of us. Iron is cold like the hearts that no longer want us. Iron is mortal yet immortal. Iron belongs outside the garden; back then, your ancestors did not need it to live. Oh, Malkin! We who were once rebel angels but never followed Satan into the pit, we who have never tasted the fruit of good and evil but yearn for human contact, oh, Malkin, we live in a world that has no need of iron. Iron, cold iron, banishes us from field and forest, from sky and earth. You think you rule it all, with iron. You can explain it all. You master the Earth and all within it, but you can never enter the Garden again, and never go into fairyland. We who are creatures of air and dream and shadow and hidden meanings, we who are the opposite of cold iron, we fade away then, we are no longer seen . . ."

"But iron is not only knife and sword and war," said Malkin, and she was weeping. "It is cooking pot and hearth and the warmth of friends. It is stories told around the fire; stories of fairyland, too, and of you. Oberon, please: iron is not only harsh."

"True, true," said Oberon's voice, and it sighed. "Iron is all things mortal. But we are not mortal. We are both greater and lesser than mortal. Malkin, Malkin, in choosing cold iron, you have saved your foolish father from my Queen's just vengeance for his faithlessness and his foolishness, saved that droning, sorry creature in the glass cage too. But at what price, Malkin? Your friends do not come from the Otherland, but you do. Yet you have taken cold iron itself into your heart. Where do you belong now?"

There was a silence. Malkin's heart was wrung beyond bearing. This had once been her place, this other country, this fairy realm. Yet she had closed the door to it. *You are almost one of us*, Oberon had said. And she had rejected her inheritance in order to do what? Mostly to save two who were, when all was said and done, of little worth indeed: Will de Montacour, who had abandoned not one but *two* children; and the Italian magician Oscuro, who had lied and cheated and who, for his own advantage, would no doubt have sacrificed Tattercoats to the Baron's obsession. But there were her friends too, who could never be truly safe in this place. And Tattercoats, who was more than friend to her—for she was her own half sister. She whispered: "Don't go yet, Oberon, please. Tell me . . . is Margaret, the Baron's daughter, living here? And tell me: why did Titania say Oscuro was dangerous, when he was just a cheat and a charlatan?"

Oberon's voice returned in a breathy sigh. "The dead are not part of our realm. We do not rule them, for we are just a part of the great world that has all realms and all life and death in it, the great world ruled by the law of heaven itself. And the magician, that drone—he is dangerous because he has a little knowledge, which he uses unwisely. Oh yes, he has powers, Malkin; he sees certain things. He knew you for what you were: stronger, more powerful than Tattercoats. In some ways you and he are like two poles of the same thing. You have used your gifts for good, for love and friendship; but he has been so blinded by ambition and greed and petty self-love that the truth may always be veiled to him. This makes him dangerous. Besides, he talks too much, and what he said came to the wrong ears."

Into Malkin's head, sharply, clearly, came a startling picture. She saw the Queen, Elizabeth, moving through the crowd; she saw the courtiers, pressing around; she saw Oscuro in conversation with the Earl of Malmsey; she saw the Earl turning, face no longer a smooth mask, keen eyes scanning the crowd.

"Yes," said Oberon sadly. "The one you saw is not only Queen Elizabeth's dearly beloved godson, he is also her spymaster. His loyalty to her is absolute. He heard Oscuro's story, which the foolish creature had absorbed whole from de Montacour, and he did not look on the girl with the eyes of a suitor, but of one who sees danger to his liege lady, for one of royal birth might attempt to usurp her power. He would not hesitate to have anyone like that watched, perhaps even arrested. The Earl is truly a dangerous man because he is serious about what he knows.

"Do not look with such stricken eyes, Malkin. The Earl's loyalty to his Queen is absolute. He would not jeopardize it for a flame-haired child." He gave a sudden chuckle. "He is one after my own Queen's heart. And now, Malkin, I must go. I am being called. I can no longer stay with you."

"Stay," said Malkin desperately. "Oberon, please . . . I want to say . . . to say . . ."

"Yes?" came the whisper on the wind. "Yes?"

"I want to say . . . thank you to the Queen. For protecting me. For protecting Tattercoats. I . . . I would give her love. And to you, too, King Oberon. For you gave us love too, I know that now. Oh, how I wish I had known that before . . ."

Now it was Titania's voice, melancholy but also light and careless, that answered her.

"Love, Malkin? Love we do not know as you do, as you speak of it. Yet you are blessed, child. You have always seen more than the others. Always that will be so. You will go far with that gift, far further than your sister or your father ever could dream of . . ."

And then came Oberon's voice, scolding, mock-dismayed, "My heart, my heart, that is not a blessing, that is a curse!" And with a peal of silvery, echoing laughter, both voices died away, echoes drifting on the wind.

» Twenty-four «

They lay in the wood, in a heap on the rotting leaves, the cart's splintered timber all about them. Malkin rubbed her head. It hurt. For a moment she had dreamed . . . had dreamed . . .

She sat up and looked about her. It was no dream. There, still dangling from her wrist, was a glass cage, gleaming faintly as if it would soon dissolve, with a frantic insect beating itself against the walls. And on the ground, along with the three companions, were Tattercoats and Will de Montacour, her father. *Stay . . .* her, Malkin's father, too.

Despair filled Malkin, and she bent her head, trying to stop the tears. She had failed in everything. Tattercoats was still in danger from the Baron, and from the Earl of Malmsey now too because of Oscuro's stupid posturings. She herself had lost the chance to regain her true home. She had realized too late that despite their strange remoteness, Titania and Oberon had loved her . . . had welcomed her . . . and she had thanked them, in her heedless, ignorant anger, by putting cold iron between them and herself. And Pug—sweet, patient, subtle Pug—was gone forever. Even the beautiful feather dress was gone.

"Malkin," said a small voice. Tattercoats was bending over her, her eyes anxious. "Malkin, I had the strangest dream." She looked right into Malkin's eyes and grimaced. "Oh, it wasn't a dream!" A smile began to creep into her expression, from her eyes to her mouth till it filled almost every corner of her kind, gentle face. She sat down beside Malkin and put an arm around her. "Malkin! Do you know what this means? We are sisters, Malkin, sisters!"

"True enough," said Will de Montacour, who was approaching them with an embarrassed grin. "You are indeed sisters. And if I may say so, each of you is a portrait of your dear departed mothers . . ." He shut his mouth hastily as both girls turned to glare at him. "You must understand," he stammered. "You must understand. I always meant well. I did not even know about your existence, Malkin. Your er . . . fairy godmother was never an easy character to understand, as you have seen. And Susanna," he pleaded, "I always meant to come back and take you away, when I had made my fortune. But fortunes are not easily made. And I thought your grandfather would . . . er . . ." He trailed off into an awkward silence.

Tattercoats beckoned him down beside them. "You must not talk so much, dear Father," she said. "You have much to learn." She took his hand and laid it over her own, then laid Malkin's over it. Malkin, watching her sister—her sister—in wonder and tenderness, met her father's eyes over her head, and suddenly she felt a strange kind of pity that was so akin to love that she knew it would eventually become so.

Gallimaufry had come forward now, hesitantly, as if unsure of his welcome. But Tattercoats beckoned him down gaily. "This is the man I am marrying, Father," she said, and the eyes of the two men—the feckless aristocrat and the Irish poet and wanderer—met, in a kind of wry challenge. Will de Montacour was the first to lower his gaze; then he raised it again joyfully.

"You two will have such a wedding, such a wedding, ah, as will be talked about for generations! For I made my fortune, you know. One night in a tavern in France, the King wagered me a goodly sum if I could . . . well, he challenged me to a contest of songwriting. You heard Tabor's song . . . well, that was it; that and other verses rather more . . . er, unsuitable for young persons' ears to hear." At this point de Montacour's face grew somewhat red, and he hurried on. "In any case the King was very pleased, and I . . . I have enough money now for us all to live in splendor for as long as we do live."

Now Tabor and Pennyroyal were approaching, and he called out, "You too, friends, you too!"

Malkin noticed with a smile that balmed her sore heart that Tabor and Pennyroyal were holding hands. Tabor said dreamily,

"My royal Penny and I need no other fortune but our willing hands and our willing hearts!"

"Yes, that is so," said Pennyroyal, giggling like a love-struck teenager. "The Queen of the Otherland never gave my Tabor a gift for his own, but I say he does not need one, for his heart always was a true one!"

All's well that ends well, thought Malkin, and she sighed. Everybody would be happy ever after, save for her. The cage jiggled against her wrist, and she looked at the violet eyes of the Italian magician gazing steadily at her. That too. She'd promised him—promised to return him to his own shape, but what kind of a hollow promise had that been? She had no magic gifts, despite her inheritance, and even less, now that she had rejected it. But she must . . . she must find a way. As if she'd been stung, she sprang up.

"We must go," she said sharply. "There is the Baron still, and the Earl, after us."

Will de Montacour was watching her closely. "Malkin," he said gently. "Titania will have seen to it that the Earl has forgotten it all by now. She can seem to be a fierce and disconcerting spirit, it is true, but that is mostly her manner, for she is deeply loyal, and even can be most tender, though she would deny it to the end. Certainly she never deserts those who have been once protected by her. And Oberon is of like heart. As for the Baron . . . well, I am here now. And I am never leaving again. The Baron must get used to me, and to seeing his granddaughter. I will tell him of Margaret, his daughter, my wife, and how I met her shade in the Otherland. I will tell him that she is unhappy because of the way her daughter has been treated. I will tell him that there is no fortune greater, no dream more wonderful, than real love. Beside that, all is cold and hard—cold and hard as iron, but not half so useful. It may not change his mind, but all we can do is try."

Malkin said flatly: "But you did not see the shade of his daughter. Oberon says the dead are not part of that realm, that they have no power over it, and so only God may make the dead rise or speak."

"No," agreed her father, his eyes still on her, his eyes pleading for what? Forgiveness? Love? Understanding? She was not sure. "I will be telling a lie, that is true." He paused, but she said nothing, so he went on: "We are all sorry creatures, Malkin, all of us mortals. We are not beautiful as dreams, as perfect as hidden meanings. We are not immortals, of whatever kind."

"No," said Malkin sadly, remembering the hall and its golden-green mysteries of light and the creatures that moved so easily in it. Remembering Oberon and Titania, creatures of dream and caprice and air and shadows. Remembering the Otherland, with its strange familiarity. It was deep within her now, that place, and would never leave her in her dreams and imagination, though she might never be allowed to find her way there again in reality.

"Father," she said falteringly, without quite meaning to use the word to one who was still a stranger to her. "Father—will you tell me about my mother one day? Will you tell me her history, how she came to be in the Otherland, and why?"

She stopped, and Will de Montacour said, very simply: "Of course, my dear Malkin. My dear daughter, I will tell you." She saw that his eyes were full of tears, and she turned away, her heart full. Her hand touched her throat, and she felt the golden heart locket still there. It sprang open to her touch and, looking into it, she saw the shimmer of the feather dress. At the same moment, she heard . . .

"Pug!" she cried, running toward the silvery sound of the pipe. And there he was, his dancing green eyes bright above the reed he was playing. "Pug! I thought you'd gone forever!"

"Me?" said Pug, taking his lips from the pipe for an instant. "Me? How can I go? I belong here. And there too. I am of both, yet of neither. Guardian and gooseherd." He grinned. "You can't get rid of me so easily, Malkin."

"But I thought . . . but I thought, that I had, with cold iron . . ." She stopped, for she understood inside herself just what Pug meant. Like her, he was of both worlds, but unlike her, perhaps his father or mother had been mortal and his other parent of the Otherland. He was a true halfling, and able to move in and out of both worlds with ease.

"The basest of metals can be transformed into gold if the heart is pure and strong enough," said Pug mysteriously, smiling.

Malkin stared at him. He had not abandoned her, he had come back into this world with her, to be with her. And she had been left the feather dress. Did this mean that she had not been rejected after all? Perhaps Titania and Oberon had known she belonged here, in the mortal world. Perhaps they, like Pug, had understood just why she had had to use the image of iron against them, because she could never be wholly a part of the Otherland. After all, Pug was not repelled by iron, was he? He was of both worlds, yet of neither: a kind of aloneness, yet a kind of greatness too. The knowledge filled her with a piercingly sweet warmth, and she was about to say something when the cage jarred violently against her wrist, and she saw the creature inside looking at her in agony. Poor Oscuro, she thought, poor Oscuro. I must, I must do something.

"Pug, sweet Pug," she cried, desperately, "will you not help me? I would free Oscuro from the spell that holds him still."

"Why?" said Pug. "Does he not deserve to be trapped as he tried to trap you? Or at least to suffer for a little while more?"

She looked at his calm face, and her heart thumped wildly. "Even if we are not powerful and beautiful as the fairies, we mortals," she said, very quietly. "Even if we are not as good and just as the angels, we are still children of God, who made all the realms of all this great and beautiful world and all in it, mortal and immortal. In us is a splinter of immortal light, as it is in the fairies and the angels. So you see, to want to trap and punish ... that is not right, not right at all."

She stopped, for she did not know how to continue, did not know how to persuade Pug. But he nodded, and she saw, with a strange wonder, that the gooseherd's eyes were shining with tears. But he said, quite calmly, "Cold iron can turn to pure gold, if the heart is pure and strong enough," and then he lifted his reed to his lips and began to play again. All at once the cage dissolved, like a bubble popping, and a man lay on the path, groaning. He looked as if he'd been set upon by robbers. His skin was of an unhealthy yellowish hue, his hair resembled a stack of moldy straw, but his violet eyes were the same. Malkin thought of how this man, in his more fortunate days, had looked on her with what she had imagined to be malevolence. Now, in that flash of understanding light, she saw that it had never been that at all, but a wariness, bravado mixed with uncertainty, aloneness mixed with greatness . . . perhaps.

Oscuro stumbled to his feet, gave her a staggering kind of bow, and said: "My Lady Malkin, I am forever in your debt. I will repay your kindness and absolve the wrongs I have done in full. I . . . I do have some small powers, but I have used them ill, foolishly. I promise that I will never do so again." His violet gaze was not quite steady, his lips trembled, but he stood and waited for her word as if awaiting the decision of a queen.

She found that at first she was quite unable to reply, for she knew she was hearing the truth—perhaps the first time it had left Oscuro's lips—and knew, too, how much it had cost the man whose cold-armored heart was now left naked and vulnerable. It was he who had been cold iron, she thought pityingly, he who had destroyed his bridge to the Otherland by his foolish disrespect. It was a disrespect, in the end, for his own talents, his own qualities, for he had been willing to demean them, to cheapen them with lies. *That* was what Titania, in all her splendid, fierce power, could not forgive.

She thought of what Oberon had said—that perhaps she and Oscuro were poles of the same thing. Her pride and his had been evenly matched, her uncertain understandings and his too. She thought of Titania's final words, that she would go far, far further than the others, and felt as if the world was opening before her. But for now there were endings to be accomplished, wrongs to be righted—and she would not be alone in doing so, would never be alone again. As Pug had said, the basest metal could be transformed into gold. Slowly she said, "Thank you, Oscuro." She found that any other words choked in her throat. Yet their eyes spoke with a kind of headily surprised understanding, a knowledge that this would not be the final word, that there would be things between the two of them that might lead to the healing of a great many things—might even lead to a love as warm and strangely right as it was amazing. Her heart hammering, Malkin tore her glance away from Oscuro, back to Pug—and saw that her friend's eyes were sparkling with an expression midway between tenderness and amusement. She colored, and frowned a little. "Is there something funny?"

"Is there not?" said Pug, and he began to play softly a tune that she had not heard before. And on the wind, she thought she heard voices she recognized, singing words that she had not known before, but that seemed familiar in the depths of her being. She took up the words, gently humming, then joyfully roaring at last, the others joining in; and so filling the woods with music, they took the path that would lead them back to Fisher Forest.

> Gentles, do not reprehend;
> If you pardon, we will mend:
> And, as I am an honest Puck,
> If we have unearned luck,
> Now to 'scape the serpent's tongue,
> We will make amends ere long;
> Else the Puck a liar call:
> So good night unto you all.

» Afterword «

This novel draws its inspiration from many sources: the English fairytale *Tattercoats,* William Shakespeare's lovely play *A Midsummer Night's Dream,* Elizabethan history, and the traditions of fairies and fairyland, which occur all over Europe and which are a long way removed from our modern ideas of fairies as little things with wings.

In general fairies were seen as inhabiting a parallel world to ours, the "other country" or "otherworld." They were not usually small but human-sized, they often had relationships with humans, and they sometimes snatched children from homes. These children were then known as changelings. Usually humans who went into the otherworld had all kinds of prohibitions put on them, such as not speaking. Some humans were welcome in fairyland and were able to move in and out of it, especially musicians and poets, as fairies love fine words and music. Fairies were neither good nor evil; most often they were capricious. They could give great rewards to those they liked, yet often punish others severely from mere whim. In some areas, such as Scotland for instance, fairies were seen as rather dangerous—an interesting account is given in an extraordinary book, first published in 1692, Robert Kirk's *The Secret Commonwealth of Elves, Fauns and Fairies.* In other countries, such as in England, feelings were more mixed. Who were they, and what did they represent? No one is sure, although more recently some people have seen them as nature spirits, or transformed versions of mythological characters, or memories of pre–Iron Age tribes, or even the dead.

The traditions I have particularly drawn on for this book are the English ones: from the writings of the medieval writer

Ralph of Coggeshall, who spoke of a changeling child called Malekin; to the traditions recorded by the great English folklorist Katherine Briggs, in books such as *The Vanishing People* and *The Anatomy of Puck*. The fairies in my book are characteristic of how they were seen in Elizabethan times. The idea that cold iron is a protector against fairies is a very old one, although it is a tradition never fully explained in the old stories. (It is also one of the reasons, by the way, why people used to nail up horseshoes on doors.)

The songs in the novel are mostly of my own invention, but "Hey Ho to the Greenwood" is by the great English Elizabethan composer William Byrd; "Long Live King Henri" is my translation of a famous, and anonymous, song about King Henri IV of France; and the final song is, of course, from *A Midsummer Night's Dream*. The song "Susanna Fair," which is mentioned in the novel, is also by William Byrd.

The names I chose for my characters also came from various sources: Pug is a variant of Puck, who in Elizabethan tradition is the spirit of the greenwood, half-human, half-fairy; Malkin is obviously from Ralph of Coggeshall's book; Gallimaufry was the name used for the mixture of Irish and English that was then spoken around Dublin; Tabor means a little drum; Pennyroyal is the name of an herb. Oscuro means "dark" or "obscure" in Italian. The Earl of Malmsey never existed: he is a bit of a mixture of historical figures, such as Sir Francis Walsingham, who was Elizabeth's spymaster; and her ill-fated godson, the Earl of Essex. Tattercoats obviously comes from the fairytale, and Oberon and Titania from Shakespeare.

Ravens are often associated with magical protection. These associations date from Celtic times, from the ancient British legend of Bran the Blessed, whose symbol was the raven and whose influence is still supposed to be protecting Britain from invaders. At the Tower of London, where Bran's head is supposed to be buried, there is a large flock of ravens that is well fed and looked after because it is said that if ever they leave, Britain will be in great danger. Ravens are also associated with memory, yet they can also be birds of evil omen.

» *Tattercoats* «

An English fairy Tale, retold by Sophie Masson

There was once an old lord who lived in a lonely castle. All day he sat by the window and bemoaned the loss of his beloved only daughter, who had died in childbirth years before. Nothing budged him from his grief; certainly not the presence of his granddaughter, who was brought up quite unregarded in a distant corner of the castle. The child's father had gone away to fight for the King years before, and the old lord never once looked on her face, so that she grew up without anybody or anything. Because she was always dressed in rags, everyone called her Tattercoats. Only her old nurse cared anything for her. She would tell Tattercoats wonderful stories; the ones the girl loved best were those about the fairies.

Tattercoats's only playmate was a lame gooseherd, a lad a little older than her, who lived in a hut in the fields with his geese. This lad could play wonderful tunes on his pipe, and his music was Tattercoats's greatest joy. It seemed that the music could transport her to any place in the world: to the court or the woods, to the rivers and mountains, and to fairyland.

The years went by and by, and the old lord grew sadder and sadder, and Tattercoats grew more and more beautiful. Day after day the old man would sit in his chair by the window and weep; he was there so long that his beard grew right down to his knees and started to twine about his chair. Never once did he even think of asking to see his granddaughter, and so he grew lonelier and lonelier.

One day the King's messenger came with news that the King was to give a grand ball at the court, for his son, the Prince, had come of age and was looking for a bride. All the lords and ladies of the land were invited, and the old lord with them. So he had to get up off his chair, cut his long beard, dress himself in fine clothes, and mount a milk white horse to go to the King's court. The nurse, who was looking out of the window, saw all these preparations, and told Tattercoats, who was heartbroken when she discovered that her grandfather had not even thought of taking her with him. She sobbed and sobbed to her nurse, who grew tired of it and told her that nothing but a miracle could take her there—and that she could work no miracles. Tattercoats wandered out into the fields to see her friend the gooseherd.

"Why are you crying?" said the gooseherd kindly. When he heard what was wrong, he said: "Well, you shall go. Come with me, and we will walk to town and see what we can see." So they set off down the road, the gooseherd playing his sweetest tunes, but they had not gone very far when they met a young man on a black horse. "May I come with you?" said the young man, looking sideways at Tattercoats, who was beautiful even in her rags; and as they walked slowly down the road, the gooseherd kept playing and playing, the sweetest, strangest tunes they had ever heard. The young man could not stop looking at Tattercoats, and finally he said, "Do you know who I am?"

"Why no, Sir," answered Tattercoats, a little dismayed. "But I am Tattercoats. That is the only name I have ever been given."

"Tattercoats," said the young man, looking tenderly at her, as the gooseherd kept playing, "I am the Prince, and I am looking for a bride—and never have I seen anyone who so moved my heart as you. Will you be my wife, dear Tattercoats?"

Tattercoats looked at him in astonishment, though she liked the handsome young man well enough. She said: "Oh, you do make fun of me in my rags. Go to your ball and choose a more suitable wife among your great ladies."

"Never," said the Prince. "But so that you may see I mean what I say, come to the ball at midnight, just as you are, with the gooseherd here and his pipe and all his geese. Will you come?"

"Perhaps," said Tattercoats, and she watched as the Prince spurred his black horse on and galloped away in the direction of the town.

"Fate is not to be denied," said the gooseherd. "We must follow him." And, playing a tune on his pipe, he set off toward the town, with Tattercoats after him.

The ball was going full train when Tattercoats and the gooseherd walked in through the doors. The great lords and ladies in their silks and satins and velvets were horrified to discover that a ragged girl and a crippled gooseherd followed by a cackling flock of geese had invaded their magnificent ball. They were about to call for guards to throw them out, but the Prince walked smilingly toward them, took Tattercoats's hand, and walked with her to the throne, where the King and Queen were sitting.

"Father," he said, "this is Tattercoats. She is the only girl I ever wish to marry. What do you say?"

As the old King gazed on the girl, the gooseherd played softly on his pipe. The King sighed and said, "My son, she is a lovely girl indeed, and I can see her goodness shines out of her eyes."

"Lovely indeed," echoed the Queen, "but something will have to be done about her dreadful clothes!"

"And what does the lady herself say?" asked the King, smiling at Tattercoats.

"If you all wish it," whispered Tattercoats, her eyes on the handsome Prince, "why, then, I will marry the Prince."

At these words the gooseherd once more put his pipe to his lips, and the tune that he played was so beautiful, so sweet, that it made tears come to all their eyes. And as they listened, they all saw Tattercoats's rags change into the most beautiful clothes: a dress of shining white, seeded with pearls and rose-colored diamonds, and a mantle of rose-colored silk. The geese were turned into nine page boys dressed in blue satin, who held up her train as Tattercoats and the Prince moved into the center of the room to begin their dance. Soon the gooseherd's strange, sweet magical tune was lost in the sound of the music from the musicians in the gallery, and the couple danced all night long, not noticing that the gooseherd had slipped away unseen.

So Tattercoats became a Princess, and the bride of the Prince, and there was great rejoicing throughout the land. Only in one castle was there sadness, for the old lord never forgot his sorrow, and was never able to be as happy for his granddaughter as he should.

Tattercoats and her Prince lived happily ever after, but never again did she see her friend the gooseherd. She sent out messengers all over the country to search for him, but he was never heard of again. Yet sometimes, it is said, if you are returning home late at night, you can still hear his sweet, strange music at the end of a country lane.

ST✭R*Maker* BOOKS

StarMaker Books are about young people like you who are struggling to become hopeful, healthy adults. These young people are special and unique characters. But you will see right away that they are not perfect people. Being unique does not mean being perfect. It means discovering your unique set of God-given gifts and growing them.

Be Your Own Star!

Find out more about your unique gifts by using this visualization: Start by writing your name in the middle of the dotted area below. React to each of the five personal traits listed on the opposite page by drawing a star-point outward to reflect your thoughts. Your star-points can be wide or narrow, short or long. Label each of the five points. When you are finished, you will see your own uniqueness shining back at you.

1. **Physical:** Do you feel good about yourself physically? Draw a point to reflect your sense of how physically gifted you are.

2. **Social:** Are your relationships honest and growing? Do you have the support you need to adjust to changes within your family and friendships?

3. **Emotional:** In your mind are you an emotionally balanced person? Can you express your strong feelings like anger and fear in healthful ways? Do you know when to let go of them?

4. **Spiritual:** Do you possess a "great soul"? Do you have a sense of the spiritual, mysterious dimensions of life? Where is God in your life?

5. **Intellectual:** Do you consider yourself a wise person? Can you state your views without being judgmental of others? Do you have the gift of seeing meanings below the surface issues?

Shine On!

- Once you have drawn your starter star, the sky's the limit. Draw another star a month from now. You will find that your uniqueness and God-given gifts change over time. Color your star to say more about yourself. Make a three-dimensional star out of foil or paper. Keep it in a folder or frame so you can refer to it again.

» About the Author «

Sophie Masson was born in Indonesia of French parents, the third in a family of seven children. Her family moved to Australia in 1963, and Sophie grew up in Sydney. She now lives in New South Wales, Australia, in a mud-brick house with her husband and three children. Sophie is a full-time writer and the author of a series of young adult novels published by Saint Mary's Press.

Sophie Masson writes about herself:
My family is Catholic; my mother is particularly interested in the moral and ethical aspects of religion, my father in its mystical and symbolic aspects. Ours is also a rather lively, argumentative, and imaginative family, and we were exposed to a lot of different religious experiences. Having lived in Africa and Indonesia, I have always been interested in religion and the spiritual, and from a very early age, I felt what I call the "silent singing of the universe," which are other words for grace. I feel very strongly the idea that we are all of one flesh, one blood, and that what we do to others, we do to ourselves.

Please e-mail your reader reactions to Sophie Masson at smasson@northnet.com.au. For more information about Sophie Masson's books, contact Saint Mary's Press by e-mail at or on our web site at http://www.smp.org.